Annoying

People

Are you one of them?

Colin Scady

Dedication

This book is dedicated to all of the Italian waiters, BMW drivers, Morris dancers and others of that ilk who have annoyed and angered me for more years than I care to think about. Each and every one of them has made my life a misery.

Introduction

Do you get annoyed by certain people? I do, not just annoyed or even angry but apoplectic, furious, embittered and barely able to control my rage. There are people that make my blood boil and this book is about them. I hope that you will identify with at least some of these miserable characters and with the feelings that they evoke when I meet them. Sometimes it's their incompetence that annoys me, sometimes it's their attitude or arrogance. And sometimes these people just get up my nose by being there. All too often it's the sanctimonious garbage that spouts forth from their mouths that irks me and now and again it's simply because they are egotistical, opinionated, pompous idiots.

The people in this book are vile, reprehensible, feeble-minded, mean-spirited, shameless human beings who have outstayed their welcome. I loathe and despise them. If I were to suddenly lead a coup, overthrow the government and install myself as dictator, they will be the first to go. They will be taken to a place of safe-keeping. They will be taken on boats and by hovercraft to their new home where they will be able to spend the rest of their lives with similar minded people. Come that glorious day, they will be taken from the UK and transported to the Isle of Wight (IOW).

At first glance this might be thought to be unfair on the people currently living on this relative oasis off the south coast of England. But no, this has always been a place where the country's oddballs and undesirables have drifted to and I feel sure that they will make their new visitors welcome. It is a dead end place where, according to the results of a recent DNA testing programme, the population is all related to two people living in Ventnor. As such it is the perfect location for the worthless bunch of obnoxious ne'r-do-wells that I will be sending there.

The Island will be their prison. It is here that they will be left to get on with their own pathetic, miserable lives. They will be guarded with a 12 foot high unclimbable fence topped with razor wire. It will have watchtowers, searchlights and guards armed with AK-47 machine guns. The waters around the Island will be populated with Great White Sharks, all ferries will be banned and anyone trying to escape will be shot on sight. There will be no escape.

I am confident that you will not be surprised at the people who have been selected and that you will find some similarity between my choices, and the groups of people for whom you have a personal dislike. Who, for example, doesn't hate BMW drivers? I have never met anyone, other than another BMW driver, who has ever had anything good to say about these reprehensible miscreants. And what about dental hygienists? Is there anyone who enjoys visiting these hideous, perverted creatures? And then there is white van man - that brainless moron that you see in the rear view mirror sitting just millimetres from your bumper. You are doing 70 mph while he is eating a garage pasty in one hand and attempting to text his 'bird' with the other and still, somehow, managing to continually flash his headlights at you! These idiots shouldn't be allowed on the streets, let alone be able to drive anything on the road faster than a four year old's pedal car.

You may be more surprised by who is not included. Perhaps the biggest omission is a group of people who come in for the most criticism of any, who are the butt of all jokes and who we come up against every day - women drivers. I know that they don't signal, I know that they can't reverse, and I know that they are unable to judge the width of their car or read the road ahead. But are those good enough reasons to remove them from the face of the earth? I'm not so sure and although they may not be able to carry out these pretty basic and important elements of driving you have to admit that they have certainly mastered the art of always using their rear view mirror – albeit just to check their make-up.

I haven't included Social Workers either. So what if they only eat couscous (organic gluten free) and always wear sandals no matter what the weather; that's "cruelty free" sandals of course. Personally I've never seen a "cruel" sandal but take my word for it they exist. So what if they are all gay and members of the Socialist Workers Party. Does it matter? Does that mean that they should join the likes of Premier League footballers or slim women with a one-way ticket to the Island? No, it doesn't. I don't see anything wrong in going to Glastonbury each year or taking the odd child away from a feckless parent. Live and let live I say.

As you read through my reasoning you may think that I am being a little unkind here and there. Please do not feel even the merest jot of sympathy for any of these people. They are not just irritating they are irritating beyond compare. They have no redeeming features. They are social pariahs and they fully deserve their inclusion in this book. Do not feel sorry for them. They have brought it on themselves; they are the architects of their own downfall.

There are many other groups of people that annoy and anger me and who very nearly made it on this list. That they have not been included is simply down to an uncharacteristic generosity of spirit on my part. These people are on a final warning, a yellow card if you like. I have listed them at the end of this book and have included a short explanation of how they have achieved this status. I hope they have the sense to act on it and to become changed people. If they fail in this respect and if they ignore this heartfelt plea then I am afraid that the time for warnings is over. There will be no second chance.

The groups of people listed in this book are my choice and to a certain extent they represent my personal prejudices. If, however, you think that there are any other slime-balls out there who deserve to be joining this illustrious assembly of miscreants please let me know: scadydorset@gmail.com

CONTENTS

Final Warning

Annoying People

1   Holiday friends

Mrs Scady and I used to have some neighbours called Jean and Edward who were the most boring people ever; not just ordinary boring but nauseatingly and annoyingly boring. Jean was forever trying to barge in and help – with the children, the washing, the shopping, anything and everything whilst Edward always knew a better way of doing something (actually anything) than I did. They were both in their 80's and loved cruises. After each cruise they would regale us with details of their holiday and it was always the same story. On the first night they would meet a 'lovely couple' at their table in the restaurant but when they went back the next night the 'lovely couple' were missing and they never saw them again for the whole of the holiday. And the same happened every night. I'm sure you can picture the scene; it's a two week cruise and by the last night there are 14 couples hiding away on board, desperate not to be caught by Jean and Edward their wannabe holiday friends.

Jean and Edward have put Mrs Scady and me off cruises but we do like a holiday in the sun and every year before we go we make a detailed plan on how we can avoid being caught by a Jean and Edward equivalent. We've all met them; those hideous creatures that come up beside you when you are in the queue for food in the hotel restaurant, and say something banal like "Hot today wasn't it." Of course it was bloody hot; that's why I'm in Rhodes in August you bloody idiot. I'm here, like you presumably, for the sun. I am also here to relax and get away from the hassle of everyday life and from morons like you.

Or, on the first day of your holiday, they'll take the sunbed next to yours and just as the four lunchtime beers coupled with the heat of the afternoon sun are working their magic and you start to drift off into an idyllic world where your favourite football team wins the FA Cup, Andy Murray wins Wimbledon for the 19th time and, in my case, Mrs Scady transforms into Julia Roberts, they'll say something like "Where are you from then?" Not the same planet as you obviously and why don't you go away and annoy someone else are my immediate thoughts. But being the kind and caring person that I am I just smile and say "Dorset".

As soon as the words are coming out of my mouth I know I have made a terrible mistake. I sit up, my reverie over, and feign interest as my new found holiday friend tells me that he and Brenda, his wife, are from Hull, pronounced Ull, but they went to Dorset once.

I hear about his three children; the eldest is on drugs, the middle one and his girlfriend have just had their second child (they have only known each other for two years but .....) and the youngest has just got a job at the local pound shop. Within 10 minutes I also know that Brian (that's my new friend's name) and Brenda have been coming back to this hotel for seven years – they love it.

I don't want Brian to think that I am unfriendly and so I try to think of something I can say that he will understand. "You've got a nice tan" is the best I can come up with. He grins and tells me that they have been here since last Tuesday. These words are the most beautiful I have heard. I do the maths quickly and realise that this must be the final day of their week's holiday. "Oh great" I say trying to repress a smile of relief, "what time are you flying back tomorrow." And then it happens. Brian tells me that they are here for a fortnight. These words are the most depressing I have ever heard. I do some more maths and know instantly that Brian and Brenda will be here for the full duration of the holiday that Mrs Scady and I have looked forward to for so long.

I smile, more of a grimace really, get up from the sunbed and say something about how nice that is and make excuses about having to go and find Mrs S. I know what Brian is going to say next but even then it still hits me with the force of an out of control express train at 200 miles per hour. "Perhaps we can meet for a drink in the bar before dinner?" he says. I am poleaxed, not knowing how to respond. I want to say just two small words that mean so much - the first beginning with F and the second one being OFF and I want to say them with so much venom in my voice that there would be no misunderstanding. I want to say I wouldn't piss on you if you were on fire so why on earth would I want to spend any time with you let alone have a drink with you. I want to tell Brian that if, as a result of Armageddon, we (me and Mrs S and Brian and Brenda) were the last people on earth I would not have anything to do with him other than to say "LEAVE ME ALONE you sad bastard."

But I can't because I'm too polite. There he is inflicting pain on me of the highest order and yet I am afraid of hurting his feelings by saying that unfortunately I have a prior engagement – for this night and every other night until the end of time.

And so later that day, as the sun sets on what should have been another magnificent day, Brian and Brenda and Mr and Mrs Scady can be seen enjoying a convivial pre-prandial in the hotel bar, looking as though they are lifetime friends. And so it goes on for the remainder of the holiday.

It's the last night of the holiday that I dread most because I know that it is then that my holiday friend will make his ultimate move. I know that it's coming. I've known since day one but I still haven't worked out what to do about it or how to handle it. Normally the last day of a holiday is tinged with some sadness anyway because I know that come tomorrow it will be back to the grindstone, back to reality and back to the grim English weather. But having met some 'friends' earlier in the holiday the last night is 100 times worse; it is full of foreboding because I know what the inevitable outcome is going to be but I am powerless to do anything about it.

I know that on the last night my holiday friend is going to pass me a small piece of paper and say those words that I do not want to hear – the equivalent of my doctor telling me that I only have a week left to live. "We've written our address and telephone number down" - the paper is passed over.

"It would be nice to meet up back in dear old Blighty wouldn't it?" My hand is shaking as I take the note. My palm is sweating and I feel that I am going to faint. I want to scream, be sick, die - anything but give them my contact details. "Thanks, that would be great" I somehow manage to say. "I haven't got a pen on me but . . . "

Before I can even finish the sentence Brian, or Bill or whoever it is this time has reached into his pocket and not only produced a pen but also a little notebook for our address and telephone number. What do I do? How well do they know Dorset; he said that they had only been there once but is that just a story? Before the advent of mobile phones it was easy but now there is no excuse not to give your phone number but your address is a different matter. Do I give my correct address or do I provide a completely fictitious set of details and pray that Brian and Brenda don't spot it and that we never, ever meet again.

But they know our names and surely it wouldn't be too difficult, even for them, to search the Internet. If I am the one to receive the request I always give a false address and hope for the best. If Mrs Scady is asked she will always give our correct address because she is just too kind for her own good. And so it's game, set and match to Brian and Brenda or whoever they are called on this particular holiday and we have acquired new friends. And Mrs Scady will send them Christmas cards forevermore. The holiday is spoiled and so is my life because from now onwards I sit at home in dread of my mobile ringing or worse still of a knock on the door and it being Brian and Brenda.

Holiday friends are pathetic, miserable, needy people. They are bullies who force their way into other people's lives and they should not be allowed to get away with the torture that they inflict on ordinary people. I loathe them and I have nothing but contempt for them and their worthless lives. They are despicable people and they will be taking one final long holiday, with no return ticket. *Bon Voyage.*

2   Jehovah's Witnesses

For some reason they always seem to come in pairs. Perhaps it's for protection or maybe just support. Who cares? The key thing is that there they are knocking on my door and always at an inconvenient time. To be honest there would never be a convenient time for these most persistent of pests. The first thing I see when I open the door is their patronising smile. I despise it. And then it's "Good morning, we were wondering if ...." whilst simultaneously holding forward a copy of the dreaded *Watchtower.*

By now the door has been closed. I am always polite. I always smile as I say "No thank you". I used to think that these visits from the Jehovah's Witnesses were, at worst, annoying and the people doing the door knocking, the so-called 'Witnesses', simply a nuisance. And then one day I read some of their literature and began to realise that their visits were something far more sinister. At first I thought that they were just a bunch of people who had found God and were keen to share their beliefs with me, so that I too could live a life of joy with each day full of happiness. I thought they were driven by altruism and that they were thinking of me.

How wrong I was. From reading their own literature I began to understand a little of what they believe and why they spend their lives trying to convince strangers like me that I need to join them . . . and it has nothing to do with my spiritual welfare.

Jehovah's Witnesses are members of the Watch Tower Society and one of their core beliefs is that the world is going to come to an end and that when that day arrives just 144,000 human beings will be saved from the world's population of near on 7.4 billion. Heaven for the Witnesses is not some place up in the clouds, it will be here on Earth apparently. Like the stereotypical nutter outside the shops on a Saturday morning with his placard, they truly do believe that *The end of the world is nigh*. The problem is that they have been saying this for a 100 years or more.

Originally it was going to be 1914 but when that passed and all was fine (apart from a horrendous world war) the date was changed to 1925 and then again to 1975. After three attempts and with there being no sign of the promised Armageddon the Jehovah Witnesses have now stopped trying to prophesy the date at which the world, as we know it, will end. Instead they now say that it is more important to focus on the fact that the end *will* come rather than on when it will happen.

Anyway, when it does happen there will, according to the Jehovah's Witnesses, be just 144,000 people going to *Heaven on Earth*. These lucky few, or the 'anointed' ones will rule the earth with Christ. The remaining Witnesses will simply spend eternity in *Paradise on Earth.* Now that doesn't sound too bad to me but it's not good enough for the Witnesses; they want to be in Heaven and in charge. And to stand a chance of being one of these 144,000 bosses they have to spend their time on Earth doing God's work. Put simply they believe that if they can convert more people to their faith they will score more points with God and, therefore, He might look more favourably on them when he is selecting the chosen few to join him. I am not joking. It's target driven and just like double glazing salesmen they even have to file monthly Field Service Reports giving details of how many people they have spoken to, converted or given a copy of the Watch Tower magazine.

So they are really thinking of themselves and not you or me. How selfish is that? How un-Christian is that? Certainly enough for me to keep closing the door when they come-a-knocking.

The Witnesses have a lot of other beliefs, some perfectly fine and which most of us would agree with but they also have others which I think the average man or woman in the street would think are barking mad. They do not believe in lying or stealing. They do not approve of violence or war and they think that the killing of animals for sport is wrong. So far, so good.

But they also do not approve of unchaperoned dates! This is the 21st century but if you're a Witness you are not allowed to go out with someone of the opposite sex without a third person being present just to make sure that you are not doing anything you shouldn't – like kissing. It goes without saying that they do not agree with sex outside marriage but did you know that they also do not believe in drinking alcohol (it soils the mind), gambling (the work of the Devil) or masturbation (more soiling of the mind, as well as the sheets presumably!). The more you read about them the more you realise what a bunch of miserable spoilsports they are.

Of a more sinister nature is their stance on education. They actively discourage their members from *over*-educating their children. They are happy for them to have the minimum of learning but they do not want people to be able to think for themselves.

They say that higher education is pointless and that spending time preaching the Witnesses beliefs is all that is needed. They see education as a threat to their very existence.

It's widely known that they do not celebrate their own or their children's birthdays. In fact they don't even celebrate Christmas, acknowledged across the Christian world as the birth of Jesus. The only thing they believe in celebrating is the death of Jesus. Cheerful bunch aren't they and what a great party that is for sure. And of course they absolutely refuse blood transfusions, preferring to die rather than commit what they say is a sin. Again the more you read about this bunch of nutters the weirder they become.

Jehovah's Witnesses are convinced that their particular form of religion is the right one; that they are the only ones correctly following God and that all other religions are flawed. The Witnesses are a club like no other club. You are certainly not allowed to marry anyone who isn't one. It is simply not permitted. And if you decide that being a Witness is no longer for you, well think again. If you leave you are shunned by your family and friends for life. You are totally ignored and you effectively become a non-person. They call it disfellowshipping. You don't need to leave the religion to be disfellowshipped. If you break any of their rules, for instance if you smoke a cigarette or have sex outside of marriage you will be shunned.

If you fail to repent your sins you will be disfellowshipped. You might think that two of the founding principles of any religion are forgiveness and compassion and in most cases you will be right but not with this group of self-serving, mean-spirited loonies.

To paraphrase the great Bill Shankly, some people think that the Jehovah's Witnesses are a dangerous cult, a secret sect that swallows up weak and fragile people. But actually they are far worse than that.

I can promise the Jehovah Witnesses that on my first day as dictator they will finally get the Armageddon that they have been foretelling of for so many years. Their long wait will be over. They should be aware, however, that my version of Paradise on Earth will be very much different to theirs. Paradise for me is a world purged of these holier-than-thou creeps and their evil beliefs. Paradise for them is the Isle of Wight.

3   The Scottish

Scotland is a fantastic country with snow covered mountains, deep glens and wondrous lochs. The weather is bloody awful but the countryside is wonderful. I love the place and there is no doubt that it is one of the most beautiful parts of the UK – apart from the people. The Scots are an abject bunch of misfits. They walk around with a glum look on their wind and rain beaten faces waiting for an opportunity to moan about something. The Scots will moan about anything. Indeed it's their most popular pastime north of the border and the subject they like to moan about the most, the one that is ingrained into the very fabric of their body and mind, is the English.

It's strange really because there are so many of them living and working south of the border in a country they hate, with people they despise. Go into any pub in England near to closing time and I guarantee that there will be at least one drunken Jock, propping up the bar. He'll have a chip on his shoulder bigger than Ben Nevis and he'll be spouting on to anyone unfortunate enough to be in his presence about how wonderful Scotland is, about how much he misses it and how much better it is than England. My response to this is FOBTT, shorthand for F*** Off Back There Then.

One of the other problems with the Scots, and there are quite a few, is that no one can understand what they are saying. They speak the same language as you and me but you would not know it. They have taken the Queen's English and destroyed it beyond recognition. The Scots use words that don't exist and they put words together that shouldn't be anywhere near each other. When they speak every word slurs into the next to such an extent that they sound drunk when they are sober, and after a few drams, as they are prone to saying, they are completely unintelligible. What other race would say '*Lang may yer lum reek*' when what they mean is '*May you live long and keep well*'? The answer to my question, of course, is '*I don't know*' or '*Ah dinnae ken*' in their particular argot. My favourite phrase, and the one that sums up the Scottish language perfectly, is '*Yer bum's oot the windae*' which translates as '*You're not making any sense.*'

Nowhere is this ridiculous excuse for a language more evident than in the poems and writings of Robbie Burns, arguably Scotland's most famous son. For some reason that only makes sense to the Scots this man is revered as the godfather of Scottish culture and his poems continue to be quoted by drunken Scotsmen the world over.

Burns is best known for writing the song Auld Lang Syne, a dirge that we thankfully have to endure just once a year – and once is far too often for me. One of his most famous poems entitled *To A Mouse* starts with the following verse:

> *Wee, sleekit, cowrin, tim'rous beastie,*
> *O, what a panic's in thy breastie!*
> *Thou need na start awa sae hasty,*
> *Wi' a bickering brattle!*
> *I wad be laith to rin an' chase thee,*
> *Wi murdering pattle!*

Beautiful stuff I think you will agree. If this was supposed to be nonsense verse like Edward Lear's wonderful *The Owl and the Pussycat*, it could almost be tolerated. But Burn's words are to be taken seriously or so the Scots say. They compare him to Shakespeare and like nothing more than to analyse his words for their hidden meanings. Hidden meanings, my ass. Burns is no more than a con artist and his trashy poems are fit for nothing other than the incinerator.

Another reason for including the Scots is that they eat some of the most disgusting food in the world. We have all heard of the Scots like for deep fried Mars bars and deep fried pizza but these two delicacies are nothing compared to some of the more traditional dishes. How about trying *Festy Cock* or *Cock a leekie soup*, *Fatty Cutty, Rumbledethumps, Granny sooker, and Strippit baws.* And what self-respecting Englishman has failed to retch at the sight or smell of the national dish – haggis. What sort of person is it that takes the heart, liver and lungs of a sheep, mixes them with onion, oatmeal, suet, spices and salt and then encases it in the stomach of the self-same sheep before cooking and eating it? The only person who does this is a Scotsman. It sounds revolting and it is revolting and it is certainly not food.

There is something strange about the Scots and their need to do weird things with the parts of animals that most of us would prefer not to think about. Take that other symbol of Scottishness, the bagpipes. That they sound like an abomination goes without saying. That grown men have been known to cry at the sound of them and that children have nightmares at the merest mention of them is a given but did you know that they are made from the skin of a small goat or sheep.

The holes from where the unfortunate beast's legs once protruded are used to fit around the pipes and the whole thing is encased in pigskin. Again, who would do such a thing? Who ever thought of doing such a thing? You know the answer - those good-for-nothing, haggis chomping, caber tossing numpties from beyond Hadrian's Wall.

The Scots are the only race on the planet where the men wear skirts and the women wear trousers, or trews as they insist on calling them. There is something very ridiculous about a man in a kilt. There is no need for it and there is no logical reason for it. So why do they do it? The origin of the kilt is supposedly linked to the Scottish weather and to the Scottish habit of fighting the English. It rains a lot in the Highlands and if you wear a kilt you apparently stay much drier than if you are dressed in trousers like 99.9% of the world's male population.

The kilt, so they say, also gives you more freedom to run over the boulder strewn landscape whilst at night it can be removed and used as a blanket. Well, that is the official version according to Lady Nancy MacCorkill. Personally I don't believe a word of it. If your diet consists of the aforementioned *Festy Cock, Fatty Cutty* and *Rumbledethumps* I have a sneaky feeling that you might need to be going to the toilet a little too often and very quickly and if you were wearing trousers there would be too many accidents.

When I was a teenager I absolutely hated whisky. I was told that it was a wondrous drink and that I would acquire a taste for it as I got older. A lot of years have gone by since then and I still detest the stuff. It is the only alcoholic drink that I dislike and no wonder. Drinking a Scotch is like pouring a mixture of petrol, ear wax and gorilla urine down your throat. I correct that; it's actually worse.

There is no finesse about a Scotch whisky. It's, crude, harsh, unsophisticated and rawer than your bottom would be if it was dragged naked over burning hot coals. I actually don't think that anyone truly enjoys the stuff. Being able to drink a neat whisky is taken as a symbol of manliness; you're not a man until you've downed a bottle of single malt without once allowing a grimace of pain to take over your face. It's a badge of honour and it's a con.

Scotsmen are renowned for being "tight" with money. According to received wisdom all Scotsmen have short arms and long pockets. They call it being thrifty. Everyone else calls them tight bastards and the stories of Scottish meanness when it comes to spending money are legendary. There's the story of the Scot who makes his wife heat the knives so that they use less butter or the Scot who, on his way out to the pub, told his wife to put her hat and coat on – not as she thought because he was taking her with him but because he was going to switch the central heating off.

And finally what about Scotland's perpetually under-performing football team? They have proudly entered the European Championship on 14 occasions and they have proudly failed to qualify 11 times. In the World Cup they have never ever progressed beyond the 1st round. It truly is a dismal record that has provided their supporters (the ridiculous Tartan Army) with nothing to cheer about over a period of 50 years or more.

I am always ready to see the best in people but with the Scots there is no 'best'. They are a strange race. They are dour, stingy and prone to eating the parts of animals that common sense would tell them to stay away from. They have a language that's not really a language but more like a secret code devised by a band of drunken gerbils, and an army that consists of grown men dressed in skirts who travel around the world cheering on their fellow countrymen as they embarrass not just themselves but their country. The Scots have earned their one-way ticket to the Island.

I am not, however, proposing that all Scots make the journey. The chosen ones are the drunken, mind-numbingly boring Jocks that have left their home country to live in England. In what can only be described as an uncharacteristic act of generosity I will allow all the Scots currently living north of the border to remain there.

4   Old People

There are so many things that I dislike about old people that it's difficult to know where to start. What about their clothes? Why do they all wear beige trousers made of a material that looks as though it should be on the outside of the space shuttle? Not just beige trousers but beige trousers with an elasticated waist, pulled up almost to their chest. It's awful. And what is it about their hair? Older women always have stiff-as-a-board, immaculately coiffured hair as if they go to the hairdresser every day. Perhaps they do. Perhaps that's how they get their kicks. At their age they are not going to get them any other way. The men, of course, have more hair sprouting out of their ears and nostrils than on their head and it's gross. Haven't they heard of mirrors and nasal hair trimmers?

Old people are always going on about the past. It usually starts with "*In my day ..*" or "*Did I ever tell you about . ..* " Yes you did you stupid old sod about a zillion times and it wasn't interesting or funny the first time. They will invariably tell you that we don't know how lucky we (the poor unfortunate younger person that they have pinned against the wall) are.

They didn't have mobile phones; they didn't even have an ordinary telephone, a fridge, freezer, washing machine or a bathroom.

And that explains why old people always smell. They don't wash their clothes and they don't wash themselves. They also smell for other reasons. They have no control over their rear end and nine times out of ten if they bend over to pick something up, or simply get up out of a chair, they fart. Worse still they don't apologise. Of course they don't because they either can't hear or they think that just because they are old they have the right to do what for most of us is socially unacceptable.

Another thing that annoys me about old people is that they are always moaning about something. The weather is usually too hot or too cold, it's too windy or too wet. Whatever the weather they are unhappy with it. They are always moaning about the television; the fact that there is nothing on worth watching. This is despite that fact that they have a 100 plus channels to choose from when "*in their day*" there was only one. The crucial issue here, of course, is that they can't even turn the television on without help and once that's done they can't use the remote control. It might as well be Dr Who's sonic screwdriver.

Old people are always getting in the way. Wherever they are, whether it's on the footpath or in a shop they shuffle along at a speed that a snail would be ashamed of and all the time they are completely oblivious to everyone and everything around them. You're in a hurry and you try to sneak around them and they veer off their straight line so suddenly that you fall over as you try to stop yourself running into them – well you wouldn't want to touch them would you? On the road they are 10 times worse. It goes without saying that they never get out of first gear. That they are slow drivers I can forgive but I cannot accept that that they have to drive in the middle of the road holding you and dozens of other motorists up. Eventually after 10 miles you manage to get past, you look at them willing them to look back so that you can shout at them – to tell them that they are a bloody awful driver and that they should not be allowed on the road – but they just stare straight ahead. You have been behind them for an hour, you have waved, you have flashed your headlights but they have not seen you once.

There is something about old people and food that I just do not understand. Why is it that none of them like pasta, pizza, peppers or anything with a "*foreign*" sounding name? Did they never like these foods or does becoming an old person change your taste buds?

Perhaps when you get to become an old person the government sends you a list of how you must behave. As far as food is concerned that means that you only like offal or cottage pie, except on a Sunday when you must have a traditional roast dinner – but only on a Sunday. Whatever food they are eating, old people always eat painfully slowly (they do everything at the same ponderous pace) and of course they complain about the size of the meal – it's always too big. Is there nothing these people like?

Old people think they are wiser than young people. They think that simply because they have lived longer they know more. The fact that most of them can't remember where they live or what year it is doesn't matter. They are older therefore they are wiser. They also think that just because they are old you have to respect them. How can you respect some doddery old git with piss stains on their (beige) trousers and the remains of a meal eaten three days previously stuck between their teeth.

Old people are also very rude to other people. They seem to think that just because they are old that can say what they like. It doesn't matter whether it's a waitress or a doctor. Old people are rude to everybody, even to each other but their greatest hate is reserved for young people who they treat like a piece of shit. They do so and get away with it because there are no repercussions; no one argues with them and no one tells them that their behaviour is unacceptable.

It's a fact of life that as you get older your health deteriorates. Age brings more health problems and more visits to the doctor and to hospital. As a result old people talk endlessly about their ailments, illnesses, operations and bowel movements. Never ask an old person how they are. I guarantee you will be stuck for an hour as they tell you about the open sore on their legs which is constantly oozing puss, about the catheter they have just had fitted and about their piles which they have to push back up their scrawny, poo stained bottom on a daily basis. Old people also talk about funerals because at their age their friends and colleagues are popping off on a daily basis and their own death is about the only thing they have to look forward to. They monopolise our GP's time and they take up beds in hospital which are needed more urgently by younger people. Old people are a drain on the health service.

So let's summarise what we have here. Old people have appalling dress sense, they don't wash their clothes or themselves, they go on about how wonderful it was back in their day, they are rude and hate young people they do everything at a painfully slow pace and even if they were aware of the annoyance, frustration and anger they cause among other people they wouldn't give a damn.

Old people are terrible drivers, they dislike any food that begins with P, they piss themselves and worse and it costs the rest of us a fortune just to keep the cantankerous old wankers alive. And on top of all that they think that they are so bloody clever.

No contest surely. Let's do them a favour and let's do the rest of humanity a favour. They are included and when the glorious day arrives they will be taking their place alongside the other misfits in this book to await their fate.

5   Politicians

No explanation is surely needed for these odious creatures. This bunch of low-life, this group of privileged ne'r-do-wells are surely on everybody's list and not just on the list but at the very top. Ironically this is exactly where they see themselves – at the top of the pile and this, in itself, illustrates exactly what is wrong with politicians. They believe themselves as some sort of superior race. They often consider themselves above silly things like laws which the rest of us have to abide by and, of course, they have three other distinguishing features. They are unable to give a straight answer to a simple question, they are pathological liars and they have a virtually insatiable appetite for money.

Integrity and honesty are just two of the qualities that most, if not all of us, would expect of our politicians. These are the people, after all, whom we elect into a position of power and authority and who we choose to do the right thing for our country and for us. Unfortunately these are the very people, who from their well-publicised actions, appear to have no integrity or honesty whatsoever.

Let's look at this in more detail. Everyone knows that, for reasons known only to themselves, politicians rarely give a direct answer to a question and all too often they are even unable to answer a question that requires a simple Yes or No answer. This was beautifully illustrated in a BBC Newsnight interview between Jeremy Paxman and Michael Howard, the then Home Secretary in the Conservative government.

Howard was being asked about his involvement in the sacking of the governor of Parkhurst Prison and whether or not he threatened to overrule the Head of the Prison Service.

Paxman: "Did you threaten to overrule him?"
Howard: "I was entitled to express my views. I was entitled to be concise"

Paxman asked the question again and received the same non-reply. All Michael Howard had to do was to answer Yes or No but did he? Did he hell. By now he was looking pretty stupid. Even my dog who was watching with me was beginning to realise that Michael Howard was trying to hide something. Most of us would have given up by now which is, no doubt, exactly what Michael Howard was expecting.

But this was Paxman. He asked the question a total of 12 times, and 12 times Michael Howard blustered, obfuscated and generally ignored what was being asked of him. This was a senior politician, a Secretary of State, elected by the people, holding a position of great importance and yet he refused to give a yes or no answer to a very simple but important question. Quite simply it was disgraceful.

The utter greed of MP's was brought to public notice by the Daily Telegraph in 2009. For years apparently MP's had been abusing their extremely generous allowances and expenses system to the tune of millions of pounds. A Freedom of Information request revealed that MP's were claiming for second homes that they were either not living in or which were just a few miles from their main home and that others were claiming for a mortgage on a home when it had been paid off many months before. Did they own up? Did they say sorry? Did they hell. Their excuses were all much the same. As one miscreant said when he blamed a member of his staff it was "an unforgiveable error in accounting procedures." Who was he trying to fool?

To furnish these second homes MP's were allowed to claim £10,000 for a new kitchen, £6,000 for a bathroom and £750 for a television. The rest of us have to save up to buy these things or do without them completely but not our politicians. If they want something they can claim for it – from public money, our money. There were reports of one MP claiming expenses for 16 bed sheets, two flat screen TV's and two DVD players – all for his one bedroom flat! The greed of politicians knows no bounds.

In 2015 the avarice of two former foreign secretaries was caught on camera in a huge sting by Channel 4 and the Daily Telegraph. The Conservative Malcolm Rifkind claimed that he could provide "access to every British Ambassador in the world" for a price. He explained that his fee for half a day's work was "somewhere in the region of £5,000 to £8,000." He obviously considered himself worth more than Labour's Jack Straw who proudly explained: "So normally, if I am doing a speech or something, it's £5,000 a day, that's what I charge." Can you believe it? Back in the 19th century Lord Acton famously said that "Power tends to corrupt and absolute power corrupts absolutely". Never has this been more true than when applied to politicians.

These people are not exactly on the breadline, scraping around for every penny. In 2016 an MP's basic salary was just a few pennies short of £75,000 a year. You will note that this is their "basic salary". This can be bumped up for all sorts of reasons depending on what role they have. Cabinet Minister's, for example, receive around £135,000 a year.

Compare that to the national average annual wage of just £27,600. In 2016 the national minimum wage was £7.20 an hour or just under £15,000 a year for a 40 hour week – some five times less than what an MP earns. And that's without their expenses. In 2014 our 650 MP's claimed a whopping £106 million or £163,000 each.

But it's still not enough. In 2016, if you can believe it, a government minister quit politics for good because he and his family just couldn't live on his annual salary and expenses of £120,000. Don't you just feel sorry for the poor soul and the other 649 struggling to make ends meet? Struggling to get by on more money in a year than it takes many of us five to ten years to earn. I certainly do not feel sorry for them. I have nothing but loathing for them and their seedy, rancorous view on public life.

The greed and arrogance of MP's is unbelievable. It is astounding and it's a disgrace and for those reasons they rightly earn their place on the Island.

6   Facebook Users

I am an infrequent user of Facebook (FB) but although I am not on FB every week I have used it enough over the past few years to know that FB users are the most crushingly tiresome, bullying, sanctimonious, opinionated, offensive, self-obsessed, politically fanatical, insensitive, partisan and manipulative idiots that you could ever wish to meet. And its regular users, the ones who are on it at least once a day are the worst. Mrs Scady is addicted to FB and but for her thrice daily FB fix she would find it nigh on impossible to get through life.

FB users are detestable for a number of reasons but mainly because of the inane and egotistical posts that they insist on making. Recently, for example, Margaret one of Mrs Scady's lady friends posted a beautiful photo of herself looking far more glamorous than she ever does on a day-to-day basis. The woman is a dog and I do not mean one of those adorable King Charles Spaniels; more like a cross between a Bulldog and a Rottweiler. How she managed to doctor the image I do not know but doctored it obviously was as anybody who knew her could clearly see.

And yet almost immediately I could see that people were pressing the Love button and leaving messages such as *'Aww hun, you're so beautiful'* and *'Wow, you look great today.'* Margaret, of course, believes these ridiculous lies and her already inflated ego has now reached gargantuan proportions. I cannot understand why these people didn't just say what they were thinking, what I was thinking. If they were Margaret friends why didn't they tell the truth – that she was never going to be beautiful and that she is a deluded and miserable old woman?

I have seven FB 'Friends', all of whom are men. Mrs Scady has 473 Friends. I do not know who they are but I do know that they are full to overflowing of their own self-importance. They are, without exception, contemptible people. I know this because I often look over Mrs Scady's shoulder as she pounds the keys. I have lost count of the times that these imbeciles post how wonderful their children are (usually because the little shit has managed to clean his or her own teeth or some such banal activity) or what a crap day they have had; typical reasons being that they had to wait two minutes for their skinny latte or they couldn't get the right shade of lip gloss.

One Friend insisted on sharing every poooomp, poo and piss emanating from her new baby, and this was after she had regaled everyone with every puke, pelvic pain and push of her pregnancy. On top of this there was how few hours' sleep the yummy mummy had managed to grab, how she was far too tired for sex and how she only just managed to fit in her nail treatments. As if this wasn't bad enough, this continued every single day for the whole first year of the baby's life and then she damned well got pregnant again. She obviously wasn't that tired!

The 2016 EU referendum really brought out the opinionated bigotry of Facebook users, with the self-styled intelligentsia smugly assuming that the common people couldn't possibly win the day. They were laughing on the other side of their smug little faces when Mr Farage came up with a family-sized quarter-pounder grin on June 24th.

The 'remainers' used their Facebook clout to make any 'outer' feel like a pariah and from that moment forth being branded an 'outer' was possibly worse than being a Nazi amongst my group of seven FB Friends. '*I hope you feel ashamed of yourselves*' was one of the nicest intelligentsia' comments, whilst '*burn in hell*' was more common.

Some of the comments were really unacceptable and they were all aimed at making me and the other 15 million who voted to leave the EU feel bullied. Colin Scady is made of sterner stuff however. My response was simple. Get over yourselves, this was a free vote in a free country and just because you didn't like the outcome does not give you the right to abuse the sensible majority who voted that way.

If FB had an 'exterminate' button, I would be pushing it continuously, ridding the world of the brainless jerks that put up posts such as '*Major tragedy in my house today, don't know how I will cope.*' Nearly everyone replies by pressing the 'sad' emoticon and they say something like '*If there's anything I can do to help…*' or '*Oh babe, private message me please, I am so worried about you*' or '*Feel for you whatever's going on*'.

The person who posted has succeeded in their attention-seeking mission. Just wise-up everybody, if there had really been any sort of tragedy this numbskull would not be on FB. Normally these creatures are female and the catastrophe is something to do with false eyelashes, broken nails or a spot appearing on their nose. I hate to say it but some of the culprits are also men; their problem being that their tickets for the big match didn't arrive in time or they damaged one of their alloy wheels. Attention seekers are the low-life of FB and should be ignored.

Our niece is in a class of her own when it comes to FB. She appears to live her life through her FB posts which cover every subject under the sun except politics; that key omission being because she comes from Basingstoke and doesn't understand civilised society let alone how the country is governed. The niece is a big one for photos and shared banners and she manages to offend Mrs Scady with most of them. Last week's picture was of a monkey with a downturned mouth and upturned nose with the caption '*The look on my aunt's face when I walk in the room.*' If I am honest I could see the resemblance but Mrs Scady was not amused.

On another occasion she cancelled Mrs Scady from a babysitting assignment only to then put up a post saying '*massive thank you to my friend Annabelle who stepped in to babysit for me tonight after I was let down.*' She puts up photos of her baby almost every day and is probably making the poor little devil the most hated babe in the world just by ramming him down everyone's throats. When she does anything vaguely commendable with her other children (like baking cakes) everyone has to see it on FB and acknowledge what a wonderful parent she is – yuk!

We are all being manipulated into thinking that this little saint of a woman is carrying the world on her dainty little shoulders. It really sucks and FB is to blame.

Facebook is an out-of-control monster which is bringing about the end of society and I honestly believe that Mark Zuckerberg is Satan's disciple on earth. But at the end of the day it's the people who use FB who are to blame. Without these dumb, feeble-minded, arrogant maniacs and their squalid posts it would not exists. Their days are numbered.

7   Chuggers

If you have never heard of a chugger you will certainly have met them. Chuggers are people who are paid to collect for a particular charity. Chuggers are the people who harass you on a Saturday morning when you are out buying a newspaper. They are usually young and they will wear a brightly coloured T shirt with the name of the particular charity that they are working for that day emblazoned on the back. They'll carry a clipboard and they work in packs, like hungry wolves, making it almost impossible for you to pass by. If you're male you will be attacked by a girl chugger and if you are a woman the attack comes from a boy. I say attack because that's how it feels and that's how they get their name – chuggers. It's short for charity muggers and that's exactly what they are. Let's not mince our words, a mugger is a thief and chuggers are thieves.

If they were simply waving a collecting bin and asking for a few coins, like the majority of normal street charity collectors, that wouldn't be a problem. But the chuggers want more than that. They start by simply trying to engage you in a conversation. It could be about the weather or about something in the news. But once you have stopped you're hooked.

Their next tactic is to go straight for the killer blow and ask what you think about children starving in Africa, or suffering from war in the Middle East. It's not necessarily always about children. It could be about elephants being killed for their ivory or the plight of homeless people in Manchester. The key thing is that it's a massive tug at your heartstrings. You are not going to say you don't care are you.

And that's where the clipboard comes out. Their one and only aim is to sign you up to give a regular monthly payment to the charity they are being employed by and a payment by direct debit. They are not interested in asking for a few coins; they want the big bucks that come from a long commitment, because they know that once you have signed up you are unlikely to cancel your direct debit and certainly not in the short term. The charities have done their research and they know that once you are hooked the average time that you stay making your monthly payment is three years. According to a chuggers handbook published online people under 18 year of age should be avoided because they are more likely to cancel their direct debits and generally the older the person the longer they are likely to continue their giving; older people either forget or just can't be bothered to stop their payments.

So it's not the charitable causes involved that I have a problem with. It's the methods used by the charities themselves. I am not even blaming the chuggers because they are only doing what they are paid to do. But having said that it is these over-enthusiastic, aggressive, deceitful, shameless young people that will suffer, come the revolution.

Most chuggers have never even heard of the charity they are working for until their first day of work. They are generally paid the minimum wage but they receive a commission for every person they sign up on a direct debit. Chuggers are in it for the money and it's the commission that motivates them.

It's not great work but if you don't mind flirting with a complete stranger, if you have no qualms about giving someone a guilt trip or if you just enjoy fleecing someone of money that they might not be able to afford then being a chugger can bring great rewards. Some are reportedly making up to £1,500 a week. With that sort of money available it's hardly surprising that chuggers will go to any length to sign you up. They will tell lies, they will deceive you and they will not give a damn as to whether or not you can afford to give the monthly amount that they are persuading you to sign up to. "Would you like to save a child's life? It's only the cost of a cup of coffee a week" they say, "and you're putting an end to malnutrition in the third world". Yeah and I also believe in fairies, is my usual response.

Chuggers are a pest. They invade your personal space. They are emotional blackmailers and they care not one jot about you or about the charity they are collecting for. They only care about themselves and their commission and they will not let anything or anybody stand in their way. They are no better than double glazing salesmen; they have to close the deal and they will hassle you until you sign on the dotted line.

I do not think that I could ever be accused of being judgmental but Chuggers are despicable people doing a despicable job. There are much better, more dignified ways of collecting for charity and chugging should be banned by law. Unfortunately it is still legal and so it's the chuggers that have to go. I have no hesitation in including them, along with BMW drivers and Italian waiters, in the list of super annoying groups of people to join the exodus to the IOW. I see it as charitable act.

8   Young People

There are so many things that I dislike about young people that it's difficult to know where to start. What about their clothes? Why do they all wear a baseball cap the *wrong* way round? If any young people are reading this let me tell you that the peak is at the front – that's the part of your head where your eyes and nose are. You wear a baseball cap with the peak at the front to protect your eyes from the sun. If you wear it back to front you look like an imbecile, you look as though you are on temporary release from a secure institution and it is certainly not cool, or hip or sick or whatever the word is that you use to describe something good.

And why do they wear a hoody pulled over their head even when the temperature is 30^0 c and walk around with a hunch back that would make Quasimodo look like a stiff backed regimental sergeant major? Young people (of the male variety) also insist on wearing jeans that either have a crotch that is barely two inches from the floor or with the waist around their backside so that their underpants are showing; that's the top of their designer pants, the bit with the name on which is almost always Calvin Klein.

Young girls are no better. They seem to think that, no matter what size they are, they have to wear a thong, most of which is on show above the waist of their jeans which like their male counterparts is nowhere near their actual waist. It isn't pretty and it certainly isn't sexy on a bottom the size of a baby elephant's.

And what is it about their hair? Young women always have vivid pink, blue or green hair; it's as if they have dipped their head in a bucket of fluorescent ink. Perhaps they have. Perhaps that's one of the ways in which they get their kicks. The boys, of course, either sport the obligatory Mohican or a number two all over with some obscure symbol etched in. If they do have a normal head of hair it always looks, to use a phrase of my mum's, *as if they have been dragged through a hedge backwards*. Each strand of hair is going in its own different direction. Haven't they heard of mirrors and combs?

Another thing that I hate about young people is that they adapt to new technology faster than a Formula 1 racing car can get from 0 to 100mph. No matter what it is, from hardware such as the X-box, PlayStation and smart phones to social media like Twitter, Facebook and Instagram, they take about half a Nano-second to understand how it works.

And once they know how something works they use it all the time. Why are young people *always* on their bloody mobile phone? If they are walking along the street the phone is either glued to their ear as they take part in some utterly banal conversation or it's held in front of them as they wildly pump in a text message, finger and thumbs a blur as they pass on a no doubt crucially important message to some other young idiot. Why do they feel the need to be in constant communication with each other?

Another thing that annoys me about young people is that they are always moaning about something. If they don't have a job they moan about that, even though their ripped jeans, ridiculous hair, inability to utter a coherent sentence and general demeanour means that they are virtually unemployable. If they do have a job they moan that they are not being paid enough, fully expecting to be earning as much as a Premier league footballer even though they are employed as a temporary, part-time shelf stacker in a supermarket. They always complain about there being nothing to do and yet they'll complain even louder if they are asked to do something. They even moan about their mobile phone battery when it's flat as if it's your fault, my fault, anyone's fault but theirs.

Young people are always getting in the way. Wherever they are, whether it's on the footpath or in a shop they swagger around in gangs, arms waving frantically as though they are drowning and waving for help, and all the time they are completely oblivious to everyone and everything around them. Or are they? Is it that they just don't give a damn? They know you are there but you are not important. You are not young and, therefore, you don't count. You have no right to be there in *their* space. On the road they are 10 times worse. It goes without saying that they accelerate through each gear, to the maximum revs. That they are fast drivers I can forgive but I cannot accept that they have to weave from lane to lane, missing cars only because the other more sensible and older drivers have braked or swerved out of the way. They are maniacs and should never be allowed on the road.

There is something about young people and food that I just do not understand. Why is it that none of them like normal food like cottage pie or liver and onions or a good roast dinner on a Sunday? And why is it that they are unable to use a knife and fork. The knife becomes a dagger that is held and wielded like an assassin's weapon while a gardener would be proud of the technique that young people display when a fork is put in their hand.

They eat at the same speed as they text, and frequently at the same time. They eat as though it's the end of the world with forkful after forkful disappearing into their cavernous mouths with increasing rapidity.

Young people think that they are cleverer than old people. This is not difficult because they think that all people over 25 are stupid. They think that simply because they have youth on their side they know more. The fact that most of them couldn't tell you who the Prime Minister is doesn't matter. They are young, you are old and, therefore, you are effectively dead while they are very much alive. They also think that just because they are young everybody else has to be in awe of them. How can you be in awe of some young thug wearing filthy ripped jeans and displaying an attitude larger than the Empire State building? They think that just because they are young they can do and say what they like. It doesn't matter who they are speaking to, young people are rude to everybody, even to each other but their greatest hate is reserved for old people who they completely despise.

No one challenges them because they are intimidating and people are afraid to tell them that their behaviour is unacceptable.

Young people are annoyingly healthy. They rarely visit the doctor or hospital and they are at the peak of their fitness. As such they have no experience of the aches and pains that come with age and no sympathy for those who have.

So let's summarise what we have here. Young people have appalling dress sense, they don't wash, they are rude and hate old people and they do everything at a break-neck, dangerously fast pace and even if they were aware of the annoyance, frustration and anger they cause among other people they wouldn't give a damn. Young people are terrible drivers, they eat like animals and they dislike a traditional roast dinner. They are arrogant and intimidating and on top of all that they think that they are so bloody clever.

No contest surely. Let's do them a favour and let's do the rest of humanity a favour. They are included and I can think of no better fate for them than to have them march side by side with the other miscreants in this book and in particular with their nemesis – older people.

9 Buskers

I like music and I particularly get great pleasure out of listening to live music. Unfortunately I cannot sing and my ability to play any form of musical instrument would best be described as catastrophic. But I do have an ear for music and a tune and there are few things better that sitting in the summer sunshine with a glass of wine or a pint while listening to someone playing an acoustic guitar and singing. And if it's a song by Bob Dylan, even better.

I cannot, however, stand having my senses accosted by the caterwauling of some halfwit strumming an out-of-tune guitar who then has the absolute audacity to expect me to give him some money.

Many years ago there used to be a busker in Bournemouth called, believe it or not, Harry Potter. Other than the name he had absolutely nothing in common with the boy wizard who was to come along years later. The original Harry Potter was, without a doubt, the worst busker in the world. If I had to guess his age I would say somewhere between 80 and 192. He looked as though he lived in a cave but as it was Bournemouth I guess his home was under the pier. He always wore a jacket, shirt and tie. They, like him, had seen better days. He wore clothes that even the charity shop would refuse to take or sell. Today, of course, Harry's dress sense would be described as shabby chic.

He always wore a hat, a trilby if I remember correctly, and it obviously came from the same gentleman's outfitters as the rest of his apparel. Beneath the hat was a wizened little face, mostly covered by a swirling white out-of-control beard that looked like an elephant's nest. His guitar never had more than three cat-gut strings and not one of them was tuned correctly. To be honest that was irrelevant because Harry could play the guitar about as well as I can perform brain surgery. He strummed his three strings and just hoped for the best. The late Jimi Hendrix is renowned for getting incredible noises from his guitar but he had nothing on Harry Potter.

His singing matched his guitar playing which matched his clothes. It was bloody awful. If you came upon him you had to walk on the other side of the road because the noise was just so terrible.

There was a rumour at one time that he had been recorded by an agent from MI6, our secret services, and that they were using him to break down spies under interrogation. The story goes that the most anyone lasted was 30 seconds. After half a minute of listening to Harry Potter even the strongest willed and best trained spook would own up to anything and beg for the torture to be stopped.

The strange thing was that Harry used to make a lot of money. His hat was always full. I'm sure that most of the money came from people like me who would throw coins in Harry's direction in the hope that he would have enough money to pack up and go home. But Harry saw this largesse as evidence that people liked his performance and he just carried on giving encore after encore. Harry couldn't sing and he couldn't play the guitar but Harry was no idiot.

Back in the 1960's there was a busker called Don Partridge who actually made the big time. Strangely he, like Harry Potter, was also from Bournemouth but that's where the similarity ended. Don had some talent. He also had a personality and in 1968 his song *Rosie*, reached no. 4 in the Top 20. Don was the exception however. He could sing and he could write and with his bass drum strapped to his back he was more of a street entertainer than a busker.

Of all the buskers that I meet in the streets, the guitarists, the saxophone players, the four pretty girls in a string quartet (who are always playing to raise money to further their musical studies) the ones that I hate most are the fake Peruvian pan pipe players.

You will have seen them, you will have suffered them. These buskers come mob handed, at least six or seven of them and always dressed in what they believe the average South American peasant is wearing. If there is such a thing as an average South American peasant, that is. Big white hats, a blanket over their shoulders, brightly coloured waistcoats and lots and lots of beads. And they all play or pretend to play the most mind numbing musical instrument of all time, the pan pipes. Why pan pipes? Did you know that far from being a South American instrument they were invented by the Chinese and popularised by the ancient Greeks.

Generally this bunch of music-less impostors have never been further south than, Brighton, let alone Peru, and they always play to a backing tape. And I guarantee that you'll hear that same bloody backing tape wherever you are. It's hard to describe the sound but I'll try.

Imagine a class of 5 year old children, each of whom has a different musical instrument which they all play at once. It's not music, it's an obscene noise.

Mrs Scady likes these horrible people and their atrocious music. She thinks that it's authentic and that these con merchants are sending their ill-gotten gains back to feed their impoverished families in Machu Picchu.

Apparently she is not alone in her deluded little world; she tells me that other people like this heinous music as well. They think it has great ethereal properties and it evokes in them images of a mystical Shangri-La or high state of nirvana. I have not met any of these people, other than Mrs Scady of course, but I can only assume that they, like her, are either tone deaf, pissed out of their heads, out of their mind on drugs or as Beethoven might have said, a few notes short of a symphony. In short they are not to be relied on and their opinion counts for nothing.

What I can't understand about buskers is their arrogance. They actually believe that they can play their instrument, whatever it is, and they truly believe that they can sing. In their tiny little minds they are the next undiscovered big thing and it's only a matter of time before some fat music producer pulls up alongside them in their chauffeur driven limo, fat cigar in mouth, and waves a multi-million pound contract under their noses and begs them to sign. Dream on. The truth is that they are nobody, they are talentless and they will still be on the streets in 20 years' time. Even the very best of them make the very worst X Factor contestant (Jedward?) look and sound like a band of heavenly angels.

How do they have the nerve to perform in public? Have they no shame? Take a tip from me, never give a busker any money - not a pound, not a penny not a thing. It only encourages them. It simply helps to continue their self-delusion and that doesn't help anybody. Walk on by. Don't stop, just carry on and ignore them.

Come the day, the buskers will be there, complete with their instruments, marching along and singing their sorry little hearts out as the ferry leaves the dock.

10   Poets

All people involved in the *arts* are by the very nature of what they do self-indulgent, but none more so than poets, those writers of utter nonsense dressed up as something special. Poetry has to be the most pretentious pastime ever invented and poets the most pretentious of people. In many ways poetry, like modern art, is the Emperor's new clothes. We are told that it is creative, that it is mind expanding and that it is the highest form of artistic excellence. And it is quietly inferred that to fully understand poetry you have to be both intelligent and sophisticated.

Few of us would deny wanting to be described by these adjectives and so we pretend to understand and like poetry because the alternative is that we are considered to be a dimwit or worse still, a Philistine.

It's a huge con trick. Poetry is hard to understand because it is worthless. It is complicated, intimidating and it does not make sense. Poems do not say what they mean because poets compete with each other to use the wrong words to describe something. And the more cryptic that the poem is the more it is considered profound, mystical and full of deep meaning.

You are not meant to understand poetry. Don't just take my word for it. This is what the poet Piet Hein had to say on the issue.

> *A poet should be of the*
> *Old-fashioned, meaningless*
> *brand:*
> *Cryptic, esoteric – the critics*
> *demand it!*
> *So if there's a poem of mine*
> *That you do understand,*
> *I'll gladly explain what it means*
> *Until you don't understand it.*

Mr Hein was Danish. As well as being a poet he was apparently a scientist, mathematician, philosopher and inventor. Some people call him a polymath; my mum would have called him a clever dick. He actually 'invented' a type of poetry called *Gruk* which he said was a brief aphoristic (whatever that is) poem. I don't think that I need to say anymore. What utter bullshit.

There is a poem by William McGonagall called *The Tay Bridge Disaster* which is widely regarded as one of the worst poems ever written. This is the first verse.

> *Beautiful railway bridge of silv'ry Tay*
> *Alas! I am very sorry to say*
> *That ninety lives have been taken away*
> *On the last Sabbath day of 1879*
> *Which will be remember'd for a very long time*

I am not really the best person to comment on this but if pressed I could sum it up in one four letter word - shite. But then again I would say that about most poems. From the worst to the best; here is the first verse of a poem called *Daddy* by the acclaimed poet Sylvia Plath.

> *You do not do, you do not do*
> *Any more, black shoe*
> *In which I have lived like a foot*
> *For thirty years. Poor and white,*
> *Barely daring to breathe or Achoo.*

This is supposedly one of the best 100 poems ever written in the history of mankind. What a joke. Truthfully is it any better that William McGonagall's pathetic offering. No, it is not. It's actually far, far worse. It too is shite.

It is worse than *The Tay Bridge* Disaster because of the hypocrisy of the so-called cognoscenti who rave about Sylvia Plath simply because she committed suicide at the age of 30 and they hold her husband and fellow poet, Ted Hughes, responsible for her death. They believe what they have been told, that Plath was a distraught and troubled genius, but if they were to look at this poem objectively, not knowing that it was written by the lady herself, they would dismiss it out of hand. It would be condemned as amateurish and she would be called incompetent.

Speaking of amateurs Mrs Scady believed that she was a poet at one time. She would spend days locked in the downstairs lavatory waiting for the muse, before springing forth with her latest creation. Here is the first verse of one of her poems called *Jigsaw*.

> *I'm struggling with life's puzzle*
> *Nothing seems to fit*
> *Pieces are more difficult*
> *Nothing seems to fit*

The other 37 verses were very much in the same vein. This was one of her best attempts at poetry which, as I am sure you have grasped, says a lot about the others.

But if you really want to know why I think that poems are worthless and poets the biggest bunch of conmen ever you only need look at two poems by the American poet Aram Saroyan.

This is the first:

Lighght

And this is the second:

Eyeye

These are not the titles. These are not excerpts. These are the two poems in their entirety. Beautiful aren't they? Were you moved as much as I was?

These poems epitomise everything that is bad about poetry and its purveyors. And it's time that these sad, feeble-minded people sitting in their squalid garrets penning their preposterous codswallop wrapped up as the portal to some mind-expanding experience are brought to account.

Poems are for sissys. You need to be mad or depressed to write poetry and in a similar state to appreciate it. Poems are only truly readable when the reader is absolutely paralytically drunk. It is only then, under the heavy influence of copious amounts of alcohol that a poem begins to make any sense. Poets have had it easy for far too long and I am bringing their pretentious twaddle to an end. I will rejoice as they make their way to the Island. I may even say a short farewell.

> *Goodbye Poets*
> *If you would only know it*
> *You will write no more crap*
> *And I'll be glad of that*

11   Anglers

I hate anglers. I have no problem at all with deep sea fishermen, the brave souls who venture out in all weathers to bring back the goods for our thousands of fish & chip shops. I have every respect for them as they risk their lives for a crispy fish finger or cod bite. Not them but the other sort, the pole fishermen; the ones with a rod and a tackle box (yes, that's what it's called) and a copy of Angling Times.

I have lost count of the times that I have been walking along the riverbank or on the beach on a warm Sunday afternoon, mulling over the world's problems in my head whilst simply appreciating my surroundings and wondering at the beauty of nature. And then I bump into a fisherman.

Fishermen spoil my day with their rods and lines. They spoil my day by just being there with their exaggerated air of superiority; they look at human beings (of the non-fishing type) as though they are little better than the maggots or worms that they insist on carrying around with them. They look at us, the normal majority, as though there is something wrong with us because we aren't carrying a rod and most of all they look down on us because we have the nerve to be there, on their stretch of riverbank, harbour wall or beach. Well I have news for these sorry bastards. You don't own anything and you certainly don't own where I am walking. Get over it. Get a life you bulgy-eyed misfits.

If I am out walking by the water one of my favourite pastimes is to throw a stick into the river and watch as it's carried downstream, or skim a stone through the waves to see if I can break my record of 27 skips. Do that anywhere near to where a fisherman has his stupid fluorescent float bobbing up and down and you are seriously endangering your health. I've seen a fisherman go into an apoplectic frenzy at this, shouting, swearing and finally thrashing the perpetrator with his rod until he had to be dragged off by his fellow fishermen. I just stood there and cheered.

There are many things about fishermen that annoy me but none more than the body warmer or gilet that no self-respecting angler is without. Not the ordinary body warmer, the sort that you can buy in any clothes shop but a special one designed for fishing, the one that looks like an advent calendar.

Why does it need 27 pockets? Are they all used and if so what for? No one, not even Mr Marvel the Memory Man, could possibly remember what was in which pocket or when it was put there. I am convinced that a search of these hideous garments would reveal months-old mouldy bread, the obligatory maggot or worm and the odd rotting fish head or two.

I have tried but I cannot see any logical reason for anyone wanting to go fishing. I have a friend who is a fisherman and he once admitted to me in a moment of considerable inebriation that he regularly goes fishing and sometimes doesn't even put any bait on the end of the hook. He sits there, rod in hand, float bobbing and just drifts off into a deep trance. This is fine but there are many, much easier ways to escape from the wife, kids, dog or even mother-in-law which do not involve you taking a folding seat, three fishing rods with stands, a bait box, a landing net, an umbrella, fishing reels, weights, floats, hooks and other paraphernalia? Why would anyone want to take this equipment with them and then sit still, moving only to re-bait their hook or take a bite out of a garage sandwich that was purchased on the way? No sane person, no one with an ounce of common sense, would do it.

Do these degenerates fish because they are hungry, starving and they need to put food on the table? Absolutely not. Many anglers throw the fish back in the river once it has been caught and many fish are virtually inedible. Do they fish because they consider it a sport? If so how delusional can you get? In my eyes sport is a contest where each participant generally has a more or less even chance of winning. Where's the sport in a 'contest' between the most intelligent creature on the planet (man), armed with the most expensive and sophisticated equipment versus a fish? Answers on a postcard please.

No, people fish because they are socially inadequate. Fishermen are losers, Billy no-mates and cranks. They should not be allowed to despoil the countryside with either their own miserable bodies or the ton of fishing paraphernalia that they are always accompanied by. The day is fast approaching when the riverbanks, harbour walls and beaches of our country will be free from this menace.

12   Hairdressers

If there was to be a priority; if a group of people were going to be the very first against the wall then hairdressers would be up there with the best (or should that be worst) of them. They have so many irritating habits and annoying characteristics that their inclusion in this list was automatic. Unless you have been born with some genetic disease that stops hair growth it is safe to say that you, like me, will have experienced hairdressers at their most excruciatingly worst. So much so that I hardly feel that I need to justify their inclusion. I'm joking.

First, why the hell are they interested in holidays, or more specifically my bloody holiday? Depending on the time of year I absolutely guarantee that you cannot go to a hairdresser without being asked either "Are you going anywhere nice this year?" or "Have you been anywhere nice this year?" And whatever you say in answer to this question, whether it's Majorca or Machu Pichu their reply is invariably the same. "Nice." And then after a pause of exactly 4.3 seconds "I've always wanted to go to . . . Majorca or Machu Pichu" or whatever.

There is then another pause. They wait because according to hairdresser etiquette you, as the customer, are expected to ask one of the standard reciprocal questions. "What about you?" Or "Have you been anywhere?" The answer is always the same – they're going to Magaluf/Falaraki/Ibiza in a week's time and they are VERY excited. Before you can nod, which is to be avoided at all costs unless you have a yearning to walk out of the place looking like a Mohican Indian (scissors are a dangerous thing in the hands of a hairdresser), they then regale you with the full story. From booking the holiday three months before to having to buy a separate suitcase for all of their makeup, and of how Kev (their other half) is taking a bottle of HP sauce because he hates foreign food.

As I say why are they interested in other people's holidays? Did they get the wrong career advice at school and are they really just frustrated travel agents? Come to think about it did they get any career advice at school? Did they go to school? If this is not the case perhaps they simply get some weird vicarious pleasure out of listening to a complete stranger tell them about a bar in Paphos where they got rat-assed on barrel wine and the Moussaka was served by someone called Maria. Don't they know that all the bloody waitresses in the Mediterranean are called Maria?

But it's not just holidays that hairdressers feel obliged to talk about. They are absolutely obsessed with just talking – about anything. Well it feels like anything but go to the same hairdresser enough times and you will soon find out that there are just five subjects. Why do they feel that it is necessary to engage their customers in banal, mindless conversation? I go to the hairdresser reluctantly. I go because my hair is growing; it's over my ears and I'm beginning to look like a paedophile. I do not go there to talk about holidays, my job, their job or where they are going on Saturday night. I do not want to talk. I want to sit there quietly, grimacing as the scissors do their work, hoping that they'll get it right this time and I'll walk out looking and feeling better than when I went in. Fat chance.

I once found a salon where the hairdressers actually ignored the customers and simply talked among themselves – incessantly. It was heaven. I adored it and then one day I turned up to find it had closed down due to a lack of business. It seems that some people actually enjoy the banal conversation that inevitably comes with a visit to the hairdresser.

Take my tip. Don't ever go to the hairdresser mid-week. This is, again, guaranteed to elicit standard question no. 2 from chapter 13 of the Hairdressers' Handbook entitled

'Encourage the client to talk about themselves', it makes them feel good and usually leads to a good tip. "Not working today then?" Does it look like it? No, I'm either on holiday or I don't work because I don't know if you've noticed but I'm sitting here in this chair with a filthy table cloth around my neck listening to you.

I always lie to this question. Usually I say I'm a zookeeper. Inevitably this brings a hush to the salon as your hairdresser is thinking to themselves "what do I say next?" and the others who have been listening in think "Thank God I didn't get him". You can feel their thinking process; you can almost hear the pages of the Hairdressers' Handbook being turned over until the right section is found. And it always is. You will never nonplus a hairdresser. They will never ever be found wanting for what to say for longer than seven seconds.

So we talk about my job, about shovelling huge piles of gorilla poo (this always brings a "sooner you than me" chorus from hairdressers one and all), about working in the reptile house (my favourite job and one assured to result in the hairdresser dancing like a poorly operated marionette – arms and legs going in four different directions – accompanied by screeches of uuugggghhhhhh). And, in a whisper, about the time I had to help the bull elephant inseminate his mate. This kills the conversation stone dead and we move on to something else – within seven seconds of course.

You might think that I am exaggerating about there being standard questions that hairdressers are taught to ask of their clients. I can assure you that I am not. In 2016 there was an article in The Times about '*conversational etiquette at the hairdressers*' which quoted the *Hairdressers Journal* as saying that there were certain questions that every hairdresser should learn; 1) Have you been on your holiday, 2) Any plans for the weekend, 3) Where did you last have your haircut, 4) Did you see the X-Factor / Big Brother / Strictly Come Dancing?

I could go on . . . and on . . . and on about hairdressers but that would hardly be fair. There is limited space in this book and there are many other people that I need to write about, other equally annoying people that it would be wrong to exclude. But before I conclude this tale there are two further points that I just have to mention. Failure to mention these whilst talking about hairdressers would be the grossest dereliction of duty.

Firstly, why is it that they are totally incapable of estimating measurements, be they imperial or metric? I sit in the chair and they ask what I want. I resist the natural reply "A haircut please" and say something like "Oh just a tidy up" or "Just a trim please". To which their reply always and not unnaturally is "How much would you like off?" This is where we start running into problems. I say "Oh just half an inch please." Why I don't learn I do not know. Imperial measurements were abolished about 20 years before most of today's hairdressers (or certainly the ones that I frequent) were born. They look at me with a blank stare as if I have suddenly started speaking Urdhu. "About 12mm I say." They continue to stare before seizing the initiative and grasping a hank of my hair and asking "About this?"

At this stage I am amazed because the length of my hair sticking out from their beautifully manicured fingers is, even to my best guess, about as near to half an inch as you could get without actually getting a ruler out. "That's great." I say and relax back in the chair. And then, of course, they proceed to cut and cut again and again, and again. It's a bit like an artist who is never quite satisfied with what they are painting. They just have to keep going. Well, that's fine with paint on canvas but not with my hair. The half inch is eventually transformed into at least two inches and I walk out of the shop looking like a cross between a skinhead (remember them?) and a new recruit to the US Army Marine Corps.

Mrs Scady's daughter went once to her regular hairdresser for a trim. She asked for no more than a quarter of an inch to be taken from her luscious, long, locks. In between receiving the instructions and wielding the scissors there was an unfortunate disconnect in the hairdresser's miniscule brain. She started at the back. It was beautifully and stylishly done. The daughter looked down at the 12 inch long tresses on the floor and said that she hoped that this wasn't her hair. It was. There were tears from the daughter and tears from the hairdresser who said that she thought the daughter was the previous customer, a wannabe punk wanting a no. 2 all over. The repercussions went on for more than a year.

For that alone hairdressers are included. They have done their last blow-dry and they will bore no more people with their mindless questions and pointless conversation.

13   Italian waiters

Or more accurately waiters in Italian restaurants, here in England. And not just Italian. Waiters in French and Greek restaurants are not much better but it's those smarmy, dark skinned, smooth-tongued lotharios from the land of Michael Angelo that I detest most.

You go to a restaurant with an English waiter or waitress and what do you get? Service, that's what you get, good unobtrusive service. Your order brought to your table when you want it, hot if it's supposed to be hot, cold if not. Wine poured just at the right time, dishes taken away without you noticing it, and sometimes even a smile.

But dare to visit an Italian restaurant and it's completely different. Obtrusive service with the waiter interrupting every conversation, when they bring the bread, and then at two to three minute intervals when they return to ask about drinks, then wine, then water, and then your order. This, of course, is just ancillary to their main job. Which is smooth-talking your wife, girlfriend or whoever else you are dining with, as long as, of course they are female.

Age doesn't come into it either. You could be with your 97 year old grandmother, with her rotten teeth and smelly breath but within seconds these Lambretta driving, pizza making pests will have charmed her pants off! This even happened to Mrs Scady on the one occasion that we visited our local trattoria, proof indeed that there is not one ounce of sincerity in their preposterous patter.

And it's the same old patter, no matter who the waiter is and no matter which particular Italian restaurant you are in. You have heard it all before. More importantly your dining partner has also heard it umpteen times before and yet they always fall for it again. Why? What is it about these silver-tongued Latins that makes all women suddenly turn Blonde?

If you are there with your girlfriend or wife, its: "Senorina, you are very beautiful, bella, bella; Eeese these your papa? No, imposs...ible, you lookaa too young to be his wife. [this is always accompanied by a lowering of the shoulder and a wink] No, no, no, I donna believe it."

If you are there with your mother it's: "Senorina, you are very beautiful, bella, bella; Eeese these your boyfriend . . . your brother? No, imposs...ible, you looka too young to be his mother [this is invariably accompanied by a shrug of the shoulders]. No, no, no, I donna believe it."

And if you are there with your wife and her mother it gets even worse: "Senorina, [aimed at the mother in law] you are very beautiful, bella, bella; Eeese these your sister.
No, imposs...ible, you looka too young to be her mother. No, no, no, I donna believe it." Then a look to your wife and "You ...a very lucky Senorina. Your mama issa very beautiful. Bella, bella. Looka what youra gonna be like in a [a look to you with a smirk that only you catch] 30 yearsa time."

What utter drivel. You cringe as you hear each and every word dripping out of their mealy mouths. You know each syllable, let alone word; you've heard it all before a thousand times and so has the woman you are with and yet she still falls into a swoon as if she is a virginal, naive 12 year old on her first holiday in Sorrento. By that I mean innocent but there is nothing innocent about their reaction. You can actually see your wife/girlfriend/mother in law* relax; they slip back and if it wasn't for the chair back they would, within seconds, be horizontal on the floor, eyes glazed over and almost drooling.

"Ooooh", they swoon. "No, this is my boyfriend/husband/daughter*."

* Delete as appropriate.

It's at this stage that you know you are lost. The waiter, who is now your biggest enemy, also knows this and it's very important that you remember this. Forget it at your peril.

And then of course there is the dreaded *pepper mill*. At probably every other type of eating establishment in the world you table will come with not just crockery and cutlery, possibly even a small vase with a flower in it, and at night a candle; it will also come with condiments. From the greasiest cafe with its cheap, plastic, and often dirt encrusted, salt and pepper pots to chic Bistro pubs with their open pots from which you take a pinch of Dead Sea salt and ground Madagascan pepper corns (and which you know contain seven different traces of urine) to the grandeur of the Ritz's silver and cut glass art deco works of art, your table will have its very own salt and pepper.

But not in an Italian restaurant. Oh no! That would be too simple. In an Italian restaurant your meal comes, served as you expect with smarm but then, instead of tucking in because that is what you are there for after all, you have to wait. You wait, with a mixture of anticipation and dread.

You wait for the smarmball of a waiter to appear. You know he's about to arrive five minutes before he actually does because you see the end of a ridiculously long pepper mill come over your left shoulder like the giant one-eyed-trouser-snake it's supposed to represent.

'You lika summa pepper Senorina?' And once again the woman you are dining with appears to collapse into a state of total and overpowering compliance. The waiter has them in the palm of his greasy Latin hand. And you hate him!

But there's more to come as he twists and turns and screws. By now no one is watching the freshly ground pepper as it falls seductively over the pasta. The food is irrelevant. The waiter and your dining partner are gazing longingly into each other eyes and you feel like a voyeur in a trashy novel.

And the most annoying thing about it all; the thing that really gets up my nose and makes me want to shout and spit and swear. It's not the waiter with his fake tan and false Italian accent. It's not even that the woman you are with has turned into a complete idiot. What really pisses me off more than anything is that more often than not, the food is absolutely bloody delicious. *Porca miseria* as they might say!

14   BMW Drivers

In German it's the Bayerische Motoren Werke, in English the Bavarian Motor Works and all over the world it's abbreviated to BMW. These cars are the epitome of German engineering and they ooze luxury and quality. And in the UK BMW own and make the marvellous Mini – a fantastic car that combines style, comfort, performance and quality. What can be wrong with that? Well, nothing really; it's not BMW cars I hate, it's the people driving them. I prefer to know these by my own three letter abbreviation, SBD – Smug Bastard Driving.

For an awful lot of people owning a BMW is the ultimate aim. It's what they strive for working 60 hours a week in a job they hate just so they can save enough pennies to buy their BMW or Bimmer as the real aficionados love to call them. These are very shallow people. Compared to them a newly formed puddle is the Marianas Trench.

But each to their own and if owning a BMW does it for them then who am I to criticise. Let them get on with it. And I would but they are not on this list just because they own a BMW (although that is a major factor in its own right); they are here because of the way that they drive as soon as they are behind the wheel of a car with the BMW badge on the bonnet. They are here because of their attitude and it is because of this that I cannot forgive them.

BMW drivers assume a certain look which shouts "I am driving the best car in the world [in their worthless opinion] and I have arrived [that's what you think you useless shit]." It's not that they look down their nose at anyone driving anything other than their cherished Bimmer it's that they just don't see anyone else. If you are not one of them you do not exist. If you are not in their club you should not be on the road.

This becomes very obvious when you come face to face, or bonnet to bonnet, with a BMW at a space on the road where one of you has to stop and give way to let the other through. It can be in the town and the problem could be a parked car or it can be in a narrow country lane. It doesn't matter because the result will always be the same. The BMW driver will never give way, not even when driving etiquette suggests that he should (it's almost always a he). Why should he? He is driving a BMW after all. In his tiny mind he is driving the most sought after car in the world.

There's no recognition of the predicament in which you each find yourself. There is no friendly smile. There is no look behind his shoulder to see if there is a space for him to reverse into – and there always is, immediately behind. There is nothing. No response at all other than smug arrogance that you can sense, that you can almost see, enveloping his car like a protective mist.

So you end up reversing 50 yards, around a couple of blind corners, with the ever present danger of meeting something coming up behind you at speed, until you find the tiniest of spaces that you somehow squeeze into. And then what happens? The turd in the BMW goes past you without giving you even the slightest of thanks. No wave, no smile, no lifting of the hand, not even a raised finger as a mark of his appreciation. Of course not, because he's driving a Bimmer. You should not be surprised (but you always are) because he's an SBD.

I should say here that I have, on one occasion, been in this situation and the driver of the other car, a BMW, actually did reverse into a space behind him to let me through. I was so amazed that as I passed by I had to stop and thank him. We both wound our windows down. I explained that BMW drivers just do not give way to others and that by doing so he had destroyed all my preconceptions concerning BMW owners. "Oh, it's not my car" he said. "I just borrowed it, I normally drive a Skoda."

It's on the motorway or a fast dual carriageway, however, that BMW drivers show their true colours. This is where their arrogance and self-righteousness is displayed at its beautiful best. That they feel the need to flash their headlights at you goes without saying. It doesn't matter what lane you are in, they want you to move over so they can pass. They could, of course, simply move out into an overtaking lane but that would be too easy. Why should they anyway? You are in their way, they are driving a BMW and you are not.

And if you have the temerity to actually overtake a BMW that's when the fun really starts. The SBD will immediately wake up from his reverie. He has been affronted and you cannot be allowed to get away with it. His ego has been dented. And don't forget BMW drivers have an enormous ego so there's an awful lot to get dented. He has two options. He knows it and you know it. He either changes down a gear puts his foot down hard and overtakes you before disappearing into the distance or he pulls in front of you so close that you have to put both feet on the brakes. Either way it's the reaction of a shit.

I am not the only person who thinks that BMW drivers are the worst on the road and that they are rude, bad tempered and dangerous. A study reported in the Daily

Mail in 2013 found that the most aggressive drivers on the road were those sitting behind the wheel of a blue BMW. They were the drivers most guilty of road rage and the drivers most likely to ignore traffic regulations.

It doesn't matter whether it's a stop sign, a no parking sign, a no overtaking area or a red traffic light. The rules of the road that we all have to obey do not apply to the pompous half-wits sitting behind the wheel of a BMW. If they want a coffee or if they have to collect their tuxedo from the dry cleaners they will just stop. It doesn't matter if there isn't a space, they'll just double park and block the road. They are BMW drivers and they have a right.

But the main reason for including these assholes here, the real reason that I loathe and detest BMW drivers is because they actually think that the rest of us are jealous. They judge us by their own misbegotten standards. Just because they see owning a BMW as the pinnacle of achievement, they think we are envious of them because we can only afford a Nissan Micra or whatever.

It's not in my nature to make snap judgements but BMW drivers are stupid bastards. I pity them. I feel sorry for them. They are the ultimate narcissist and their time is coming to an end.

15   Cat lovers

I actually like cats. If I was to going to have a pet it would almost certainly be a cat. But cats and cat owners are different. Cats are delightful. They are soft and friendly. They sit on your lap purring and they just love to be stroked. Cat owners are maniacs and without exception they are disturbed and obsessive human beings. Cat owners also always look like their cats; they have evil eyes.

I lived next door to a lovely old lady called Ethel once. I didn't know anything about Ethel but she was obviously a refined lady down on her luck. Her voice was what my mum would call posh and her clothes clearly defined her as being upper middle class. Or they would have at one time. When I knew Ethel she rarely washed and she wore the same clothes week in, week out. They, like Ethel, were a little threadbare and in need of some soap and water. She reminded me of Mrs Scady.

I could live with all that. It caused me no problem and if she wanted to walk around looking like Mr Stink's wife that was her choice and I respected that.

The problem with Ethel was that she was a cat owner; more than that she was a cat lover. Ethel shared her dilapidated bungalow with 200 furry friends.

I think she gave up on men after the Second World War and she decided to invest all her energies in cats; they were her life's work. She provided sanctuary for the lame ducks of the cat world and boasted three-legged cats, one eyed cats, bald cats, incontinent cats and cats that made a tiger seem like a pussy cat. At night Ethel would go out amongst the warehouses of south east London and 'rescue' feral cats to add to her family. Some of the cats lived indoors with Ethel and others lived in centrally heated huts in her garden –huts that were significantly superior to most of the makeshift houses in Soweto or in the Favelas of Rio De Janeiro.

The smell of these 200 or so cats wafting over the fence between our two gardens was nose-breakingly bad, a 24 hour a day stench of cat piss and shit. Bad enough you might think but cats, of course, are no respecters of boundaries and within no time at all my garden was a cat toilet. Is there anything worse than stepping into a pile of fresh steaming cat shit? Of course there is but even so it's not a hobby that I recommend to anyone. My first reaction was to want to strangle each and every one of those bloody moggys – before delivering Ethel of a similar fate. I didn't of course. As a good neighbour I went next door to talk to her.

The house was like something out of a horror movie. The stench of cat pee was overwhelming and I had to cover my mouth and nose with a scented tissue even to go inside. Ethel was seated in her cramped kitchen with her ulcerated legs oozing under their bandages. These bandages were being licked by a particularly evil looking black cat whilst his compatriots occupied the adjacent settee, the sideboard, the bed, the coffee tables and the window ledges.

As I sat talking to Ethel I was being watched by at least 60 pairs of eyes – they were not welcoming eyes and their malevolence was frightening. As I tried to get out they barred my way, they scratched my legs and one of them even sprayed me with pee. What had I done to deserve this?

I tried to reason with Ethel. I explained the problem (that I was not particularly keen on dodging cat shit every time I went to hang out the washing) and gently asked if, perhaps, she could stop her feline friends from marauding into my garden, or better still could she get rid of the little bastards altogether. My pleas fell on deaf ears. In fact the normally kind and passive Ethel transformed into a demonic she-devil.

She told me, would you believe, that according to the 'Animals Act 1971', cats enjoy a unique position. She told me that cats have a 'right to roam' meaning that a cat cannot trespass and its owner cannot be legally responsible for what their cat does outside of their property. She said that her cats were, by nature, free spirits, who could not be trained to do anything that they consider to be ridiculous, like not shitting in my garden. I couldn't believe what I was hearing. I tried to reason with her but unfortunately anger ruled my brain and I screamed at her. I shouted out that she was a wanker and that her f***ing cats were evil, and that if she didn't get rid of them I would.

The next day Ethel was rushed to hospital. Result I thought, sure that this was a one-way trip. Just the cats to go. And then for some stupid illogical reason that I have failed to understand to this very day, I felt sorry for Ethel. I even felt sorry for her furry f***ing friends, to such an extent that I found myself next door feeding them while Ethel was away.

A few days later Ethel came out of hospital – in a box. Like the dutiful neighbour I attended her funeral. On the outside I was grieving; my face was as sad as sad can be and I even forced out some fake tears of sorrow to show Ethel's friends how devastated I was at her death

Inside I was jubilant, knowing that the cats would soon be gone and my five years of torture were coming to an end. It was at the wake that I heard that Ethel had left her home to a cat charity and that they were actually going to extend it so that they could look after more of the vicious little monsters. The cats had won. I had no choice but to capitulate and the For Sale sign was outside my house the next day.

Before moving into my next house I made absolutely sure that none of the neighbours for 50 yards either side were cat owners. I first checked for cat flaps and found not one in sight. I then spent many a night, all night, watching their properties to see if there was any feline presence. Again I found none at all.

Two days after I moved in a cat appeared on my front lawn. I watched incredulously as it assumed the position, shuffled backwards and deposited its unwelcome package on my neatly manicured grass. I was apoplectic with rage and stormed out of the door wellington boot in hand which I threw with all my might and anger at the offending moggy. Just then my immediate neighbours arrived home. It transpired that the cat was a stray which they had taken in just a week before and intended to keep. My nightmare was beginning again.

Needless to say my neighbours were not interested in my predicament. They couldn't care less about their cat shitting in my garden and told me that the problem was me, not their poor defenceless cat.

And that's the problem with cat owners. They are selfish, bombastic and unctuous. They care not one jot for the hell that their little tiddles inflicts on ordinary citizens. Unlike their pets they, however, only have one life and it is coming to an end on these shores.

16   Cyclists

Cyclists are an absolute bloody nuisance and should be banned from using the road. Note the word *road*. I have nothing against those people who take part in the various cycling sports at major events such as the Olympic Games. If people get their kicks going around in circles in stupidly named events like the Keirin, Omnium or Madison then fine; it doesn't do anything for me but each to their own. As long as they stay in the velodrome they stay off this list. But only just.

Talking of strangely named events have you seen the Keirin? You could not devise a more ridiculous sport or give it a more unpronounceable name if you tried. And on top of that it's boring. In the Keirin cyclists pedal around following someone going very slowly on a motorbike for about two kilometres and then a few hundred metres from the end the motorbike goes off the track and the cyclists sprint like hell for the finishing line. Why don't they just have a 500 metre sprint and forget all about the stupid bit at the beginning? Who knows who cares?

It might be an absolute waste of time but that's hardly enough to get them off their bikes so that they can take a final walk.

And I also do not include events such as the Tour de France, where some Englishman in a yellow jersey is chased by everyone else while the French onlookers throw bottles of piss in his face. A strange Gallic custom I guess and not really my idea of a sport. Although this event uses ordinary roads these are closed for the duration of the race and the cyclists are not getting in the way of the people for whom the roads were built– motorists.

The cyclists that I am talking about are the ones who use our roads every day. These are the people who quite obviously do not believe that the rules of the road apply to them. If there's a red light, they'll pedal straight through. If there's something stopped in front of them they'll simply go up on the inside, and if they are turning left or right they never signal their intentions. These people are lethal. They take no notice of the Highway Code and they have the temerity to complain about law-abiding motorists when they frequently get hit or run off the road.

Cyclists are generally too slow and they delay the motorist on his way to work in the morning. Cyclists are sometimes too fast and they delay the motorist getting past. They don't pay any road tax, or vehicle excise duty as it's now known. And, perhaps their worst crime is that they insist on wearing clothes that appear to have been stolen from the wardrobe of some dodgy dominatrix. Not leather granted, but predominantly black Lycra with the obligatory fluorescent yellow or orange, tight fitting and very, very weird. This *uniform* coupled with their renowned bad behaviour on the road has given them the widely-used and incredibly apt epithet, *lycra louts*.

Cyclists are obsessive. They are obsessive about their bikes and they are obsessive about their weight. Serious cyclists will spend more on their bikes than most of us do on our cars. You will note that I used the plural. Different bikes do different jobs so the serious cyclist will have at least two and probably three. If you are serious about your cycling you will need a bike for sprinting, another one for general road use and a separate mountain bike for your off-road jaunts. And these bikes are not cheap - £4 - £5,000 is considered normal with £15,000 not being thought of as extraordinary.

Many of these people lead quite ordinary lives. They go to work, they get married and they have children. But they have a secret which they keep to themselves. Their cycling is in the open; their fetish for Lycra is there for all to see but the amount of money they spend on their obsession is a secret from all except their fellow sufferers.

Thousands of cyclists go to bed each night silently reciting the cyclists' prayer: '*If I die please don't let my wife will sell my bicycles for what I told her they cost*' These people are idiots. They are dunderheads and I despise them.

As for weight, the key issue here is the weight to power ratio. So once you have done your best to make your bike weigh as little as possible the only other area where weight can be reduced is in the rider. It's an acknowledged fact that cyclists are more obsessed with their weight than super models. They are, as a cyclist once said, skinnier than a heroin addict on a diet. As I say these people are idiots and they need saving from their own delusions.

If you still don't believe me perhaps the following anecdote will convince you that cyclist are in a unique world of their own.

A cyclist turned up at the regular meet with his Lycra mates but with a top-of-the-range carbon fibre ultra-high speed machine. His friends were envious and one asked "Wow, where did you get that?" He looked at them "Well I was out riding my normal bike when this absolutely drop dead gorgeous woman rode up beside me. We stopped and chatted and then without saying anything she ripped all of her clothes off and said 'take what you want', so I took the bike." His friends looked at him again with admiration in their eyes, "Well done" they said in unison, "The clothes probably wouldn't have suited you anyway".

Not all cyclists wear Lycra of course. The Sunday afternoon brigade – almost always mum, dad and their two adorable children Seraphina and Maximilian – don't wear Lycra. They wear ordinary clothes. By ordinary I mean Rohan, Ted Baker, Burberry or Vivienne Westwood of course. Compared to the Lycra louts these are a bunch of amateurs but they still manage to create the maximum amount of annoyance for the poor hard-done-by motorist. You will have seen them, riding four abreast across the full width of a quiet country lane at a little more than one mile an hour. Seraphina and Maximilian on the inside protected by their doting parents from everything the world has to throw at them. They will be on their way back from their picnic by the river, replete from their gluten free five bean salad.

Do they move over when you come up behind them? Do they hell?. Mr parent, whatever his name is, glowers at you, questioning your right to be there. "*It's a road*" you think to yourself. "*I am driving a car. I belong here. What's your bloody excuse?*" When you eventually come to a wider part of the road and zoom by you know that mum and dad are saying something completely condescending. They wouldn't swear of course, not in front of the children. And I'm thinking: "Come the revolution this lot of pretentious, hug-a-tree, middle class tossers will be on the first ferry – without their beloved bikes."

Cyclists are hated all over the world, from the USA to Australia. There are loathed so much, particularly by other road users, that there is a website dedicated to them – ihatebicyclists.com. Not even BMW drivers or the infamous white van man get that accolade. Cyclists are so hated that they are often the victims of some quite nasty attacks. In 2013, for example, a cyclist called Tobu Hockley was in the middle of a 100 mile ride in Norfolk (what fun that must have been) when he says he was hit by a car and thrown into a hedge. An accident you might think but a little later someone tweeted "Definitely knocked a cyclist off his bike earlier. I have the right of way – he doesn't even pay road tax!"

Other attacks include drawing pins and tacks spread over a dangerous part of the road causing punctures which have led to cyclists having some serious injuries, and fishing line being stretched across cycle paths in country parks, bringing riders to an abrupt and painful halt. And would you believe that it's not just drivers that find these loathsome weirdos so bad that they are driven to physical attacks.

It's not just humans either! In Australia two women were out cycling when a kangaroo bounded out of the bush jumped on the leading cyclist and then hopped off and on to her friend. Needless to say they were both shocked and injured with one of them having three broken ribs and ruptured breast implants! Strangely the first woman to be attacked said that the kangaroo didn't look angry but that it appeared to be "smiling". I bet it was. Even worse though, in the US state of Montana a grizzly bear attacked two cyclists, killing one as the other raced off for help.

If cyclists are upsetting kangaroos and grizzly bears it can't be very long before the message spreads and the rest of the animal kingdom start plotting attacks. Can you imagine the scene where a half a dozen Lycra clad pedal pushers come around a bend in the road only to be confronted by a charge of angry hedgehogs. It will be absolute carnage. It's going to happen unless we do something and for that reason cyclists rightly take their place in the queue as the first to be deported.

17   The English

The English are the most arrogant, self-centred and bigoted people in the world. They think that their armed forces are the best in the world; that their nurses and doctors are superior to all others and that in all other respects England and the English are not just better but a million times better than anything Johnny Foreigner can muster. All of this is absolute rubbish, of course. What the English do have, however, is an unrivalled superiority complex. The English invented the superiority complex.

Nothing strange there, however, because nowhere is English arrogance more annoying than in their belief that they either invented or discovered everything of any use in the world, or that they were the first to do something. So what if they did invent the steam engine, television, and the hovercraft, or even pencils and rubber bands. Big bloody deal. And who gives a damn that the English had the first postal system or the first police force. Not me, not anyone.

There is no doubt that the English were once a force to be reckoned with and that in the 18th and 19th centuries England was at the forefront of inventions and discoveries, such as the railway engine and the smallpox vaccine. But I have news for them; they didn't, despite what they might think or tell the rest of us, invent, discover or be the first at everything.

The English will tell you, for example, that the first powered flight was made in 1848 by John Stringfellow in Chard, Somerset while everyone in the world accepts that this honour was down to Orville and Wilbur Wright, two Americans who famously flew their aeroplane, The Flyer, at Kitty Hawk, North Carolina in 1903.

The English are a deluded race of people. They are supercilious shits who always think (know) that they are right and everyone else is wrong. Why else would they continue to drive on the wrong side of the road? Apart from Australia, India and a dozen or so other countries that were all formerly part of the British Empire every civilised nation in the world drives on the right hand side of the road. But not the English. Oh no. And the English are correct and everyone else is wrong, all six billion of them.

The English also still refuse to use the metric system of measurement and while the majority of the world measure length in millimetres and kilometres they continue to use inches, yards and miles. The rest of the world measures weight in kilogrammes but the English use ounces and pounds. The pint still stands as the supreme measure of beer in an English pub when all over the world they use the litre. Why? The metric system is simple and it is logical. Whatever you are measuring from distance to weight, to volume everything is in units of 10. In England people have to remember that 12 inches make a foot and 1,760 yards make a mile; that there are 16 ounces in a pound and 14 pounds in a stone. This is an archaic system which is ridiculously complicated and there can be no other reason for retaining it other than sheer bloody-mindedness.

Sport is another area in which the English believe that they excel. They claim to be better than any other country at any sport and in particular that they are world beaters at Football. Well that's what they want us all to believe. Football is, of course, a sport that the English invented. Or did they? Received wisdom says the game originated in England in the mid-19th century although there are clear records of football being played by the Chinese several centuries earlier. Worse still there are many people who will tell you that football as we know it today was first played by the Scots. Whoever invented it is immaterial. What is important is that we all know that the best football players are English and the best team is England.

Again this is a complete fabrication, a myth that the English have created and which they think if repeated enough everyone will believe. The truth is very removed from this fairy story. England has won the Football World Cup just once, and that was when they had home advantage way back in 1966. By contrast Brazil has been victorious on five occasions and Italy and Germany/West Germany have notched up four wins apiece.

In club football it's slightly better but hardly a ringing endorsement for the superiority of English football. English and Italian clubs have won the Champions League 12 times each while the real champions are Spain with 16 victories. Individually English footballers just don't rate at all. Not one has ever been voted FIFA best footballer of the year whereas footballers from Brazil and Argentina have been crowned champs on eight and five occasions respectively.

When it comes to language the English are in a world of their own. They steadfastly refuse to learn a foreign language but expect everyone else to learn and use theirs. And what a ridiculous language it is. In no other language would you have words that are pronounced the same but which are spelt differently and have completely different meanings.

Take *root* and *route*. Or *two*, *to* and *too*. And what about *flour* and *flower* and *by, buy and bye*. To make things even more complicated there are then words that are pronounced differently from what you might expect from their spelling. Words like *jeopardy*, *Wednesday*, *receipt*, *colonel* and *debt*. When it comes to plurals the situation gets even worse. The plural of *foot* is *feet* but the plural *boot* is *boots*, not beet. You can have one *mouse* but several *mice* and yet if you have one *house* you have two or more *houses*. Confused? You bet.

The English are an extremely reserved race and you would never get two strangers talking to each other. They could be marooned on a desert island or more likely stuck in a lift but they would not say a word to each other unless they had been formally introduced. The only exception to this unwritten rule is the weather. The English will talk to anyone about the weather, even strangers. In fact they will always speak to strangers about the weather. In English society it is considered far ruder not to speak to a stranger about the weather than it is to not to talk to them at all.

The English are obsessed by the weather. And no wonder. England is a part of the European continent but in terms of the weather as well as everything else, it has nothing in common with any of the other countries. England has thunderstorms and floods at a time of the year when everyone else in Europe is basking in sunshine, and they never have two good days in a row. A good day in England is one that has no rain.

English weather is so bad that it is one area in which you would think it impossible for the English to be better than anyone else and yet somehow they get a perverse pleasure out of their suffering. They even manage to feel superior about their inferior weather.

Like the weather English food has long been ridiculed all over the world. Where other countries have delicious meals created with passion from the finest ingredients the English all eat cottage pie, pork chops and roast beef. In some parts of the country their diet also includes liver and onions, pigs' trotters, jellied eels and tripe, If you don't know what the latter item is, look it up but have a sick bowl by your side. English food sounds disgusting and it tastes disgusting.

There is no doubt that the English have earned their place in this book. I do, however, have a dilemma. Not every English person is a wanker. There are some, like myself, who are perfectly normal, level-headed, fair and generous.

Additionally the Island is a relatively small space and transporting 40 million or whatever extra people there would inevitably cause a few problems. There will, therefore, be a test which every English person, me included, will have to take to determine the degree to which they are arrogant, bigoted, superior, deluded, smug, self-obsessed, stuck-up, and unfriendly, obsessed by the weather or continue to refuse to learn a foreign language. Anyone who fails this test will be deported to the island. There will be no second chance.

18   Dog Owners

Why do all dog owners automatically assume that you love dogs and in particular their bloody dog. I don't. I detest them and because of that I also detest their owners and I know a lot of people who share my feelings. Put all dog owners on a lead, that's what I say. On the end of a bloody chain leash that I can yank tightly if they misbehave – which is all the time.

If I am out for a quiet walk the very last thing I want is for some maniacal dog to launch itself at me. I do not want this animal to jump up at me and I do not want its filthy paws on my clothes, no matter whether I have been wearing them for a month or if they are fresh on that day. If I did I would have bought my own bloody dog.

And while this unwanted and unwarranted attack is taking place what is the errant hound's owner doing? Absolutely bloody nothing. OK, they will be muttering something at the animal: "Get down Sydney" or Spider or whatever other stupid name they have given it. They will also be looking at me, with a banal smile on their awful face and saying something equally ridiculous such as: "He's a bit playful" or "He likes you" as if this means that he has my permission to rip my trousers which he is currently trying his best to do. Meanwhile I am turning one way and then the other in a vain attempt to shake the thing off. But he has four legs compared to my two and it's no contest.

Dog owners will always tell you that their beloved pet has got the temperament of a saint and that he hasn't got a bad bone in his body. Yeah, sure. If that's the case why do they go into panic mode as soon as another dog is in sight? You will have witnessed it as much as I have. Dog owner number 1 (DO1) is walking along a path with his dog off the lead enjoying some free time, running here, there and everywhere. DO1 spots another dog owner (DO2) with their animal coming towards them. DO1 is now desperate to get their mutt back on the lead before it sees the other animal. Sometimes they are lucky but dogs have a better sense of smell, better vision and better hearing than their human owners and more often than not it's too late.

So dog 1 runs towards dog 2 faster than a whippet with a rocket up its backside. If they are both off the lead and they are both of the opposite sex it's not so bad. They meet, give each other a doggy smile, lick each other's not-so-private parts and either get down to business or walk away. If they are both dogs, that is if they are both male, there is a problem.

First their eyes bulge and then their lips curl back to reveal their sabre-tooth tiger like fangs. They then open their mouths wide, growling like drunks on a Saturday night in Coventry, before launching at each other.

The scenario that I love to watch in this situation is when both animals are on a lead. Your still get all of the doggy machismo plus the sight of both owners holding on tight to their dog's respective leads as if their lives depended on it - as if they were hanging on to a rope with a 1,000 feet drop beneath them - and getting redder and redder in the face. And it's always a competition between the two owners to see who has the quickest brain, who is the first to utter what everyone knows is a monumental lie: "I don't understand it. He's not usually like this." Like hell he's not.

Dog leads perform a valuable purpose; they offer some sort of control over what is essentially a wild animal. I am talking about normal dog leads, not those extendable, retractable things that an increasing number of owners are using. They are as deadly as a garrotte. You see the dog first, and then fifteen feet behind is the owner. The dog is running left and right as far as its lead will allow. It's running around people, the lead is tangling around innocent people's legs and the owner is oblivious.

I don't blame the dog. It is, as I have said an animal and is acting like an animal. I blame the owner, most of whom seem to be considerably less intelligent than their pets.

Another reason for my dislike of dog owners is that they seem to think that it's fine for their animal to lick their face and worst of all for it to lick my face. It's not and it never will be. Dogs smell, their breath smells and they dribble and I do not want them anywhere near my face. A dog doesn't care where it sticks its tongue. It could have just been licking its food bowl out, which is bad enough, or it could as we all know have had it up another dog's rear end. Dogs are animals and they have not heard of germs or disease. They find it extremely hard to grasp the concept of hygiene, and so it seems do their owners. The dogs have an excuse, the owners do not.

Dogs also seem to find pleasure in sniffing human genitalia, male or female; they do not appear to be fussy. This is both embarrassing and unpleasant and I take great exception to a dog thrusting its snout in my groin. I should say that Mrs Scady appears to be less upset about this particular element of canine behaviour than me. Dogs also have a great propensity for farting and as they have yet to understand the finer nuances of social etiquette they often do this with no regard for their surroundings.

Recently, for example, a nice lunch that Mrs Scady and I were enjoying at a local hostelry was ruined by the foulest of smells emanating from Mrs Scady's chair. Aware that she has a few problems in this area I smiled and tried to ignore it. It soon transpired that Mrs S was innocent on this occasion and that the culprit was some mangy mutt that was sleeping under her chair whilst its couldn't-care-less owners were propping up the bar. Disgraceful.

Dog owners are obsessed with dog poo. And so they should be. Dogs will do it anywhere and they do. I was once on a beach and was watching some school children putting the finishing touches to a magnificent sand castle that they had spent hours building when suddenly a huge Irish Wolfhound came bounding out of nowhere. At first I thought it was going to charge through this architectural masterpiece destroying everything in its wake, and probably kill a couple of kids on the way. But no this giant of a dog skidded to a halt like some a cartoon Scooby Doo, its paws digging deep furrows in the sand. It then turned around and backed up to the sandcastle before planting its bottom on the top turret and letting loose the largest smelliest turd you have ever seen. There it was steaming like a giant barbecue sausage.

Many years ago dog poo was everywhere, on every street corner and inevitably on the bottom of your shoes, deep in the tread stinking. Nowadays this is not socially acceptable and so-called "responsible" dog owners never take their dog out without a supply of polythene bags. They use these as gloves to pick up the offending article before putting it in their pocket like good citizens. This is absolutely gross. On one occasion I saw one conscientious owner actually holding the bag under his dog's backside and catching the stuff as it slowly oozed out. Can you imagine the feeling? Separated only by the thinnest of polythene bags you are holding a warm, fresh dog turd in your palm.

For that man's actions alone, I have no hesitation at all in including dog owners among those who will be making their final walk on these shores and just to show what a generous spirit I am they can take their disgusting animals with them.

19   Doctors' Receptionists

The stereotypical doctor's receptionist is an unsmiling, grumpy, surly middle aged woman who is totally lacking in compassion. In my experience this is a pretty accurate description of the best receptionists I have ever met. The rest, the majority, are evil vicious f***wits who spend their whole day trying, and succeeding, to piss off and annoy some very sick people.

Doctors are there to help us. They put themselves through seven years of training, suffering long hours and enormous stress just so they can fulfil their dream of making people better. Doctors enjoy meeting ill people and, like a magician, curing them. They sit in their surgery waiting with great anticipation for the next patient to come through the door, never knowing what the problem will be and not really caring as long as that person is unwell and needs their help. Doctors get a kick out of healing the sick. So why do they employ people who actually stop them doing this. Why do they employ receptionists who appear to get great pleasure out of upsetting as many people as they can; people who are already feeling like shit? And why do doctors employ people whose obvious skills and qualities are more suited to working in an abattoir than in a job where care, tact and understanding are required.

The biggest gripe that people have about doctors' receptionists concerns their obsessive need to know what your problem is. You're ill, and probably have been for a few days and you feel like death. You need to see a doctor. After the obligatory 20 minute wait listening to some crap musak because 'all of our lines are busy at the moment' and the super-annoyingly trite 'Please don't hang up, your call is important to us', you eventually get through and your call is answered. You, quite naturally and understandably ask to see a doctor and she – the receptionist - for reasons known only to her, asks what is wrong with you.

Is she a doctor? No. Is she a nurse? No. Does she have any medical training? No. Does she have an interest in medical matters; perhaps she did biology at school? Again the answer is No. She's just a nosy interfering busy-body who likes to tell her friends at the weekend about the man that came in about his erectile dysfunction or the woman with vaginal warts. It's none of her bloody business.

Doctor's receptionists have a very simple philosophy. It is that no one must get past them; they must protect the doctor at all costs. It would be a lot easier if doctors simply chained up three or four Pitbull terriers or better still Rottweilers outside their surgeries. They would certainly have a quiet life then. I guess that the only reason they don't do this is because dogs need looking after and receptionists don't.

And so they get the job done by employing women who will patronise the patient, ask personal and invasive questions and who will generally act as though they are the doormen at some sleazy nightclub. Doctors' receptionists are the Devil's disciples. They are rude, obnoxious, ignorant sociopaths and they are in this role because there is nothing else they can do. And because of this they are bitter and angry and the only way that they gain any semblance of normality, of feeling like a human being, is by venting their anger and frustration on you and me.

In common with many of the other inadequates who they will be joining against the wall it is of no use whatsoever trying to reason with these misfits. They do not operate on the same level. They are always right, you are wrong, and they will never apologise. They also never believe you.

On one occasion I had spoken to the doctor on the telephone and he had told me to make an appointment to see him that day. So I walk into the surgery, look the battle-axe behind her glass wall in the eyes and say, very politely, that I would like to see the doctor. No chance, she says. I explain that the doctor has asked me to see him. She looks blankly at her computer screen and tells me that I can't see that particular doctor for at least two weeks. I explain again.

Her face resembles the rear end of a cow as she tells me again, with the emphasis on each syllable, that I can't see this particular doctor for two weeks. She is treating me like an imbecile and I am just about to tell her to take her head out from her ass so that I can stuff the computer there when the doctor in question walks through the reception area. "Hello" he says. "It's not very busy today, come through". As I followed the doctor through the door, I turned, fixed her with a stare and thrust the forefinger of my right hand towards her in a gesture that she would have no doubt in understanding.

I fully accept that not all doctors' receptionists are bad. I have met some extremely pleasant and caring ones, and what a breath of fresh air they are. Come the day that the ferries begin to depart there will, however, be no time to differentiate between the angels and the demons. They will all be taking a short sea journey to their final destination. My message to the good ones is get out now and get another job before it's too late.

20   Northerners

Northerners, and by that I mean anyone born above a line between Bristol and London and below Hadrian's Wall, are a pain in the bum. The age old saying that it's *grim up north* is so true and the people who live there are even grimmer. The reason for this could well be that the north is awash with dark satanic mills; their chimneys belching out poisonous, black toxic smoke or it could be the weather. It rains a lot up north. Not ordinary southern rain but high pressure jets of water travelling at 90^0 to the ground at just below the speed of sound. And it's cold. Not cold like it is in the south but cold like it is in the Antarctic.

You wouldn't know that it's cold, of course. There could be two foot of snow on the ground and icicles on the end of your nose but on a Saturday night northern women will be out on the town in their finest; a skirt that would pass as a belt down south, a vest, no bra and seven inch heels. And on the terraces at St James's Park the men will be stripped to the waist singing *Howay the lads* as the referee blows his whistle to abandon the match because the freezing conditions are considered too dangerous for human life. No one wears a coat up north.

There is no doubting that they are tough up north but perhaps it has something to do with the stuff they call food but which we call waste. They eat some very strange concoctions up north such as a *parmo* – deep fried pork or chicken covered with a creamy sauce and a mountain of cheese. Another favourite is *tatty ash*, boiled potatoes, corned beef, onion and carrots cooked in milk and then mashed. Yes, it tastes and looks as bad as it sounds. And what about a *growler*, a pie in a bread roll would you believe. And who but a northerner would eat *tripe and onions* – a boiled cow's stomach for God's sake.

The main problem with northerners, however, is that they are filthy, uncouth and common. Most of them are unemployed scallys who will steal anything from anyone. It's the same wherever you are up north, from Cleethorpes to Warrington and from Macclesfield to Mablethorpe they are all working class and they think that a good night out is going to the local working man's club on a Saturday night for a game of bingo or to see some dreadful comedian and then sing some stupid drunken karaoke before filling their face with a disgusting donner kebab on the way home.

Northerners are always whinging about southerners; usually about how the southerners have all the jobs and money. Northerners have a chip on their shoulder bigger than the Angel of the North and a view on life which, like their weather, is grim.

The other thing that I hate about northerners is that they are so bloody friendly. They will talk to anyone, even complete strangers. Granted their highly intellectual conversation usually concerns the weather or how *them* in the south have stitched up the northerners again but it's still a conversation. Annoyingly if a northerner is on a bus or tram he will always offer his seat up to an older person or to someone who is pregnant. Why? What is all that about?

And of course, they speak a foreign language, if language is what it is. It is certainly not the Queen's English. This is true across the whole of the north but never more so than on Tyneside where a daughter is pronounced *dauta*, water is *wauta* and *doin* is doing. Elsewhere this wonderful argot uses *bins* for spectacles, *clamming* for hungry and *gadgie* for an adult male.

If you ever have the misfortune to find yourself up north and someone approaches you and says *giz a bag o' crisps* don't whatever you do hand over your snack. All they are saying is that they don't fancy you! And should someone say *it's a bit black over Bill's mother's* don't look around for some poor old crone with a black cloud hanging over their head. All their trying to say in their own particularly charming way is that they think it might rain. Barmy or what?

Personally I think that the government should erect a 14 foot high electrified fence between us and them up north complete with floodlit watch towers, guards armed with AK-47 sub-machine guns and dog patrols. If that's not going to happen then the minimum they should do should be to provide anyone that strays over the border from the south with a north-south dictionary or ideally a dedicated interpreter.

I am not sure whether it is official or government policy but northerners also have a different currency to the rest of the country with one northern pound being equal to around 3.3 of ours. This means that everything up north is dirt cheap. A northerner can go out on a Saturday night, have 10 pints of Boddy's and stop for a growler on the way home and when he wakes in the morning with a tongue as tasty as a bear's ass he will still have change in his pocket from the tenner he went out with.

And did I mention that northerners like a drink? It's a well-known fact that 90% of England's alcoholics are northerners. To be honest on this issue I do have some sympathy with them on this particular issue. If I had to live in some grim foreboding place where the temperature rarely rises above freezing and where the most popular cultural pursuit was whippet racing, I would be sozzled all of the time.

There is, then, a lot to dislike about northerners but what swings it for me is the fact that if you meet a northerner down south he will always be telling you how wonderful it is back home. "Up north we have better public transport, the beer's cheaper, people are friendlier and I can always get a doctor's appointment" they'll say. My response to that is the same as it is to their close compatriots, the Scottish. FOBTT (F*** Off Back There Then). If it's so bloody good up north and so bloody bad down here then piss off. For that reason alone northerners will be some of the first to make their way to their new home.

21   Art Critics

My hatred of art critics is all-encompassing; it includes all forms across the so-called arts spectrum – the performing arts such as ballet and theatre, and the visual arts. The critics of all of these arts activities are all guilty but it is the latter group – those who feel the need to share their views on paintings – who are the very worst.

They are part of an elitist clique, an unofficial club with its own language, rites and rituals. They persist in using their own mystifying argot to describe not just the piece of art – that would be too simple – but what this art means. Take these glorious examples from a review of an exhibition in Cornwall.

"*Despite its Christian origins the spirituality of this piece is universal and unrestricted by dogma, translating as a philosophical source rather than an object of worship . . "*
"*…. The loud and urgent paintings are so thrusting that one begins to wonder what, if anything, lies behind the charivari they create.*"

This is artspeak at its best/worst. Is it any wonder that I feel alienated?

I like visiting galleries. I enjoy looking at paintings but just when I am beginning to get some pleasure from a particular painting I read something like this and realise that I do not even understand what it is I am looking at, so how can I possibly like it?

Nowhere is this pretentious twaddle more evident than in reviews of the annual Turner Prize which in 1998 was won by Tracey Emin. One of her most famous works was entitled *My Bed*. And that's exactly what it was – an unmade double bed with crumpled and stained sheets. Beside or on this bed was a variety of everyday objects; an ashtray full to overflowing with cigarette ends, a near-empty bottle of vodka, a pair of well used slippers, dirty knickers and a used condom, to name just a few.

Does it sound familiar? It does to me. I've seen this all too often as, I would imagine, have most parents. It's a cliché I know but it's true; this could have been my son's bedroom on the morning after the night before except that his would have been far worse. It would have been natural and not staged. And his bed would have been just classed as dirty and untidy while Tracey Emin's was a work of art.

Her bed was, then, nothing special and yet it was very special. It resulted in record crowds at the Tate gallery and rave reviews in the newspapers. Years later it was still entrancing the critics, including Alison Cole in the Independent newspaper.

". . .   it is still a bed and all that a bed symbolises and encompasses: sleep, sleeplessness, sex in all its manifestations, birth, death and dreams . . . while its white draped and crumpled sheets have their own pictorial allure, inviting comparison with classical sculpted drapery and the unmade beds in Titian's and Manet's boudoirs."

I read this and actually started to doubt myself. Was I missing something; was this really art of the highest quality comparable to work by some of the greatest artists that have ever lived? Was I underestimating Tracey as an artist? And then I came across her explanation of how this particular piece of art was created.

"I was at a point in my life when I was pretty low – I hadn't eaten properly for maybe a few weeks and had been drinking like an absolute fish – I went out and got absolutely paralytically drunk, came home and didn't get out of bed for four days."

So she didn't set out to create a work of art. She simply behaved like my son and like a lot of other people of her age. The result of her laziness and sloth was turned into art by the critics. She had the last laugh of course. Shortly after the exhibition closed she sold *My Bed* for £150,000. Years later it was sold again for five times that amount and in 2014 a German called Count Christian Duerckheim bought it for £2.44 million. As my mum might have said someone with far more money than sense as well as a stupid name.

Nothing escapes the eagle eye and silver tongue of the art critic. The world's longest running soap opera is Coronation Street. It has been gracing our TV screens for more than 55 years and for most of us it's a take-it-or-leave-it kitchen sink drama set in the gritty north of England that follows the ordinary everyday lives of ordinary everyday people. How wrong we are. Here's a review that I came across on the Web.

"I am not I, they are not they, Coronation Street is not Inkerman Street. Coronation Street is, however, an ongoing paradigm, a speculum humanae vitae, whose cobbles incorporate the Heideggerian necessity of existence. The street qua street is no thoroughfare, it has no beginning and no end, a Ding an sich leading nowhere, but with at its still centre the Rover's, the bourne to which all travellers return. Birth, copulation and death revolve

around the old gods: Ken, whose very name means 'knowledge', an aged Silenus set against the Ewig-Weibliche, Deirdre of the Sorrows. The all-too-human plotlines are suffused with original sin — bodies remain in the concrete, love-children in others' cradles, and the commercial proximity of kebabs and lingerie scarcely needs a Freud to interpret, nor need we speculate why the factory is called Underworld. The populating she-devils would grace a Mystery play! ..."

Have you ever read anything so ridiculous? Have you any idea what he is talking about; I certainly haven't. This is verbal diarrhoea at it very worst. This is pompous balderdash that means nothing to anyone except the person writing it.

For me the whole ridiculous world of art criticism or art appreciation was beautifully summed up by the late Sir Kenneth Clarke when he said:

"I feel that one cannot enjoy a pure aesthetic sensation (so-called) for longer than one can enjoy the smell of an orange, which in my case is less than two minutes."

So, art critics of all kinds and artists themselves are in. They will be going.

22   Children in Pubs

Let's make it clear from the start. I have nothing against children in general. I like children. Many years ago I used to be one. It's just children in pubs that I can't stand. Children and pubs go together like oil and water, like blondes and brains. They don't mix and they should be kept as far apart as possible. Bringing a child into a pub is like eating a pickled onion with ice cream. Try it and you'll see what I mean.

As I said, I was a child once and back in those days children were barred from all pubs. It was quite rightly against the law. Everybody knew it and everybody respected it. Nobody complained. Back then if parents wanted to go for a drink, they left their little darlings outside the pub, gave them a packet of crisps and a glass of lemonade and told them to behave themselves and not speak to strangers. But then in the 1990's there was a change in the law and kids were allowed in a pub as long as they were in a room which didn't contain a bar. This gave rise to the popularity of the "family room" – very often a dingy ill-lit ex store-room complete with greasy tables and dirt encrusted squeezy bottles of tomato ketchup.

Over the years things became more relaxed as we copied the Europeans. "Kids are allowed to go in bars in France without any problems" people screamed. Stuff the French was my response then and it hasn't changed. They stink of garlic, wash once a month at best and eat snails, frogs' legs and horsemeat. Why would we want to copy them? But we have and we now have a situation here in England where going to a pub is like going to a children's party.

Children cannot sit still for more than three minutes; it's a scientific fact and nowhere is this more obvious than in a pub. They run around in gangs, tripping up staff and customers alike. They shout, scream and whoop like a tribe of Red Indians. And then there are the babies. There are two things that a baby is good at – crying and filling its nappy – and babies will do this wherever they are. I often pop into my local pub for a quiet lunchtime pint and a sandwich but all too often my peaceful lunch is destroyed by mewling, screaming babies and out-of-control kids running amok.

I've tried explaining this in as polite a way as I can muster under the circumstances but all I get back is abuse from couldn't-care-less parents. The landlord's not much better. Families eating bring in a big percentage of his weekly takings and he is reluctant to upset them

He's told me that he doesn't like it and he tries his best to keep the peace but at the end of the day he isn't going to ban them because they are too important. According to a survey carried out by the Good Pub Guide I am not the only one who hates children in pubs. This was the number one gripe for the guide's readers, and most interestingly from publicans themselves. They said that badly behaved children were ruining the atmosphere of the great British boozer.

My local pub has a *colouring club* where the *yummy mummies* bring their little brats to colour in stupid pictures of unicorns while they swig Sauvignon Blanc. After 10 minutes and two glasses of vino the kids are forgotten and the little shits disappear off to create havoc in another part of the pub. I've seen a child peeing in a pot plant, dirty nappies left on tables, food smeared over the carpet, and kids fighting while their moronic mothers chat about which celebrity is shagging which other celebrity.

I do not want to go into a pub and be confronted by a snotty faced two year old with its shitty nappy hanging around its knees. I do not want to go into a pub and have to fight my way around half a dozen push chairs, like a Royal Marine Commando training course, just to get to the bar.

I do not want to go into a pub and watch some lazy mother feed packet after packet of crisps into their child's mouth while they swig large glasses of Sauvignon Blanc and nip outside for a fag every five minutes. And I do not want to go into a pub to watch some snivelling monster stuff chips into its greedy mouth, a mouth that is inevitably smeared orange from the baked beans that always accompany the chips.

I go to the pub to seek solace from the world . . . and from Mrs Scady. I go to the pub to sit in silence and in the belief that I can sip my pint and read my newspaper without being interrupted. I have never liked fishing but I imagine that there are similarities between the solitary angler sitting on the river bank and the solitary drinker sitting in the corner of the pub. Both are looking to temporarily lose themselves, one in his thoughts the other in his pint.

The problem, of course, is not the children, it's their parents. Babies are nothing more than a crying and shitting machine. They know nothing more and why should they. As they grow up they turn into children and children have a low boredom threshold and boundless energy.

Take children into a pub and why wouldn't they want to play hide and seek under the tables or run around as if they were trying to escape from some evil bogeyman intent on carrying them off to wherever naughty children get carried off to?

Without a doubt it's the parents that are to blame for their children's behaviour. They and they alone have to power to control their children but they don't. Can't they remember back to when they didn't have any children, to a time not that far back when their visits to the pub were spoilt by a horde of out-of-control, anti-social little brats, screaming, shouting, fighting and generally being as obnoxious as they possibly can? Obviously not.

Ideally children should not be in pubs but if we have to accept that this is the price we pay to keep pubs alive and profitable, then these children should be well behaved. There is an old saying that *'children should be seen and not heard' and* nowhere is that a more apt rule for children than in a pub. Landlords and pub owners need to take back control. They need to make it clear to parents that they are welcome only as long as their children behave like civilised human beings, that they, the parents, show consideration for others by making sure that their children do not behave like child wild animals.

The Black Lion pub in Leighton Buzzard has the right idea. It sports a blackboard sign saying:

"To avoid accident or injury to your child whilst the little darling is running around this establishment . . . . why not hand the little poppet to a member of staff who will be happy to nail it to your table for you!"

If only Leighton Buzzard was closer. I'd be in the Black Lion every day.

Lest anyone should accuse me of misopedia and for the avoidance of any doubt I will stress that despite their totally unreasonable behaviour it is not the children who will be led out at dawn. They are young with their lives ahead of them and hopefully with the right guidance and supervision there is a chance that they will grow into responsible human beings. No, it is the parents of these out-of-control monsters that will be kissing their children a final goodbye.

23   Local Councillors

Local Councillors think they know what is best for you and me. They think that because they 'know' that they are superior to you and me and because you and I voted for them. It's more likely, of course, that we didn't vote for them and they were elected to their positions of power by a tiny minority of the people that were eligible to vote. In 2012 the average turnout at local elections across the country was just 31% meaning that in a community with 10,000 voters the local councillor would have been elected by just 1,551 people at best, with nearly 8,500 people either voting against or not bothering to vote at all. Hardly a ringing endorsement for the lucky councillor elected.

At parish level the situation is often far worse where councillors are very often elected without there even being a vote. Impossible you might think but not so. If there are 12 vacancies on the council and only 12 people stand for election they are all automatically "elected" without the need for X's in boxes or ballot boxes.

You can't blame the councillor for this of course; it's the system. But this explains why we end up with a council rammed with people who are, if I were to be kind, not the cleverest amongst us. If I were to be honest I would say that they were, without doubt, the stupidest, most arrogant bunch of misfits that you could ever wish to meet.

If you have never been to a meeting of your local council then you are missing one of the best experiences that anyone can have without the aid of mind-inducing drugs or alcoholic stimulants. It doesn't matter whether it's a large city or county council or just your local town or parish council. They are all the same. Find out when the next meeting is and get down there and I promise that you will not be disappointed.

You will be amazed, you will be dumbstruck and most of all you will probably be angrier than you have ever been in your life. Councillors are the most hideous people you could ever imagine. They are so full of their own self - importance you can feel it in the air. On the scale of smugness they out-smug even the smug bastards driving their BMW's and that I can assure you is a level of smugness that you would doubt anyone could attain. Their egos are on a par with the most egotistical egotist and they have a superiority complex that is so huge it will leave you speechless.

At the larger local authorities councillors are making decisions about spending tens of millions of pounds of your money. And they make decisions on a huge range of issues that can have a massive impact on you and your local community.

You might, therefore, imagine that these people are the brightest among us, that they have a modicum of intelligence and that they exercise their powers for the benefit of the people who put them there. You would be wrong, very wrong. Councillors are, as I have said, stupid and I have yet to meet one that possesses even an ounce of common sense. They are mostly in it for the generous expenses and the 'power'.

The other really annoying thing about councillors is that they invariably find it impossible to make a decision which is quite ironic because that's why they were elected in the first place. Councillors are ditherers and if they can get away without making a decision on anything, but particularly on an issue which is seen as contentious, they will. Councillors don't like making decisions because they don't like to be seen to upset people, and by people I mean their electorate. Councillors always have an eye on the next election even if it's four or five years away and they hate to think that they are going to lose even one vote because they have made an unpopular decision.

So they don't. They ask for a report or they ask for clarification of a particular point. They do anything they can to defer making the decision and this is the main reason that councils take forever to do anything. Councillors fail to understand that whatever decision they take it is going to upset someone, so why not get it over rather than keep delaying and delaying until they can delay no more. And by that time they have upset or angered even more people than they would have by making the decision because if there is one thing that most of us dislike it is indecision. To paraphrase Abraham Lincoln you can please all of the people some of the time, and some of the people all of the time, but you cannot please all of the people all of the time.

You would think councillors would understand this but, of course, they have not as I have said been blessed with either intelligence or common sense. You would expect councillors to have the courage of their convictions and to make unpopular decisions if they have to. The problem is that councillors, have no convictions. They are not there because they have any strong ideas or because they have an overwhelming desire for public service. They are there for their own self-aggrandisement.

These people are so deluded as to think that being a councillor gives them some sort of social cachet; that their friends cannot help but be impressed and a little envious when it is not so much dropped into conversation but made the sole subject of conversation. Councillors love nothing more than to talk about themselves.

They really are detestable people. Take my local parish council. It is chaired by a loathsome woman of dubious character whose greatest claim to fame is that she was caught shagging an eastern European who then went on to blackmail her. The treasurer looks like a paedophile and the two longest serving members are the two most obnoxious characters that I have ever had the misfortune to meet. Both of them look as though they have only recently crawled out from the primordial swamp and they both go on and on and on about how their families have been in the village 400 years and that everyone else is an 'incomer'.

For one reason or another I have attended an awful lot of council meetings – too many. And from every one I walk away laughing. Not because of anything funny but because I just couldn't believe what I had just heard or what I had just seen. I have seen councillors reading a newspaper during an important debate on social services.

I have seen councillors sending lengthy text and email messages when they should have been concentrating on the issue being discussed. I have seen councillors asleep and others, who were teachers in the real world, marking homework while all around them chaos reigned. Very often local community groups will attend a council meeting to listen to the debate on an issue that is going to have a significant impact on them; it could be a new housing development or a grant to a local children's charity, or the closing of a library. At the end of the debate these people troop out of the council chamber and without fail I have seen them look at each other in total bewilderment, asking each other what the decision was. Did we get the grant; did they agree to keep the library open; did they say yes to the new houses? Nobody knows because the meeting was chaotic.

And it's not just the public that are confused. Time and time again I have heard councillors ask each other what they decided and time and time again I have heard them say that they have no idea or give different and contradictory replies.

From reading this you may have gained the impression that I am not overly enamoured of local councillors. You would be exactly right. In their tiny misguided minds they are important because they are a Councillor. Everything about them is abhorrent

They are king amongst the most worthless people on earth. I am always reluctant to criticise anyone but Councillors are dreadful people. I have never met one who didn't have his head permanently stuck up his own rear end. The same obviously goes for the lady Councillors that I have also had the misfortune of knowing. Man or woman, it doesn't matter, they all live in their own deluded world where only they exist. Well I have news for them. They soon really will have their own little world to rule it over and it's one that they will never leave.

24   Joggers

I get extremely upset when I am driving along, minding my own business, and I see someone jogging. They may be on the pavement and they may be causing no real problem to me or other motorists but there is something about them that I cannot stand. They annoy me and I detest them and everything they stand for. I always shout at them just to let them know how idiotic they are and so that they are aware that their days are numbered.

They all have a look on their faces as if they are being tortured, as if someone is attaching electrodes to their nipples, so why do they do it? No one is forcing them. It's completely voluntary. They obviously hate it themselves but they still do it. I say nipples because the vast majority of these idiots are slim, young women. They do not need to run to lose weight. They probably don't need to do it to stay fit. They do it because they think they have to. They do it because it's fashionable and they're cool. They do it because their friends and colleagues are doing it, each of them unaware that the other is secretly hating it and taking part only because they are. It really is a vicious circle and one that needs breaking.

It's not only young women who jog of course. The other principal culprits are middle aged women (never ever older women) and old men and I hate both of these groups in equal measures. I have no idea why women of a certain age would want to jog. What do they think it is going to do for them? Do they think that jogging is going to turn back the years. Do 45-50 year old women really think that if they jog they will suddenly become 18 again? If that is the reason then they are stupid halfwits who, like their younger 'sisters', have been hoodwinked by the fashion and health industry into believing the lies that they pump out on a daily basis. They need to get a grip. They need to recognise, as my mum would have said, that they are no spring chicken anymore. They need to accept that their belly overhangs their jeans, that their tits are nearer their waist than their chin and that their bottom does indeed *look big in this*.

A few years ago Mrs Scady announced that she was going to take up jogging. A hideous image of Mrs S clad in fluorescent lime lycra flashed before my eyes. 'You silly middle-aged woman' I thought. "That's nice" I said. She lasted a week. Stupid cow.

Old men are even bigger idiots. You see them hardly able to put one foot in front of the other, socks pulled up to their knees, a ridiculous McEnroe style headband seemingly glued to their forehead and a look of confusion showing through their rictus smile. They move (I refuse to call it jog) at a speed that would make a sloth look like Usain Bolt. These people are hideous and I have a hatred for them that knows no bounds. Every time I come across one of these geriatric morons I follow them (if I am in a car this is made harder because of the snail's pace they move at – it is impossible to drive that slowly), hoping and praying that they will collapse with a heart attack. If they do my plan is to stand over them and quietly ask them if they are now satisfied before I jog off into the distance laughing.

I need to make it clear that my hatred of joggers does not extend to runners. There is a clear distinction. People run because they enjoy it. They run certain distances and they either try to better their own time or they are attempting to beat their fellow competitors. Joggers do it for reasons that I have yet to understand. I read somewhere that joggers also do it because they like cake. If that's true then that's just another reason to clear them from our streets. If you like cake, then just accept that you're going to get fat. Alternatively don't eat the bloody cake in the first place, but don't eat cake and then try to salve your own miserable conscience by jogging. These people are losers.

The other reason to hate joggers is that, like cyclists, they have their own particular uniform. It's Lycra of course, black with the obligatory flash of fluorescent pink or yellow. It is all totally unnecessary and a complete waste of money but they buy it because that's the perceived wisdom.

The right shoes are important but what's wrong with an old T-shirt and a pair of shorts? There's absolutely nothing wrong with these simple pieces of attire. In fact they're perfect for the job but they don't look the part do they? If you're out jogging because it's the *in-thing* to do then quite obviously you have to have the right gear. You have to be dressed for the part. What utter crap. As if anyone cares what you look like. You look like shit actually. If you were to look in a mirror mid-jog you'd see that for yourself but as you don't, just take my word for it.

My advice to joggers, as I slow the car and lower the window, is usually restricted to a single word – *Tosser!* Occasionally I will say a bit more. I might question their reasons for jogging or their sanity and I might ask them if they really want to live for another five years if that's what they think the benefits of jogging will be.

They don't seem to have realised that the extra five years will be added on to the end of their lives, not now. If they are 23 or 24 now they are not going to be 23 or 24 for the next five years. Logic and a simple calendar should tell them that as each year passes they'll be a year older. It's simple maths but obviously too difficult for their one-track minds.

Do they really want another five years, if that's what it is, added on to the end of their lives, five more years of the worst years of your life? Do they really want another five years of dribbling when they eat, forgetting their own names, pissing themselves or worse and being hated by the very type of people that they once were? If they gave it a second's thought I know what the answer would be. Instead of wanting to live for an extra five years any sensible person would choose to live for five years less and to do that you stop jogging – and eat more, drink more and start smoking. Simple.

But does jogging make you healthier? Will it mean that will live an extra three, four or five years? Much of the evidence suggests not.

Some very serious research around the world shows that jogging can lower your testosterone level; it can affect your immune system and can lead to critical joint problems particularly in your knee. Scientists looking into the medical aspects of jogging have concluded that someone jogging at around seven miles per hour is just as likely to die as someone doing no exercise at all. Worse than that, however, are the findings that these seven miles per hour joggers are nine times more likely to die early than people who exercised more moderately. Joggers are also being killed on a daily basis all around the world. In any collision between a human body and a car or truck you know who is going to come off worst.

Joggers really are a bunch of self-deluded, sick-in-the-head, copycat slaves to cool or whatever the current word is to describe the brainless desire to be a part of the crowd. They should be pitied I suppose, but life's too short for that sort of bullshit. They have no one to blame but themselves.

I have no doubt that come the day of reckoning these idiots will actually be the first on the ferry. Not because they deserve to be and not because they are the most hated but simply because they'll be jogging while everyone else is trying to walk backwards as slowly as possible. Tossers!

25   Footballers

First let's be clear about who I mean by footballers. I do not mean those dedicated lunatics that turn up on a cold and wet Sunday morning, nursing a huge hangover, to play for their local pub or club team, watched by two men and a dog. I don't even include the semi-professional and professional footballers playing in the lower leagues. No, you know who I am talking about – those over-paid, spoilt, sleazy, thick-as-plank prima-donnas who grace the English Premier League.

Let's start with Ashley Cole. This is the man who was married to Cheryl – key member of the all-girl group *Girls Aloud* and every man's dream. That she was gorgeous goes without saying. Sexy, you bet. Did her dad own a brewery? Actually no, but that was the only negative point. The woman was a Goddess. So what does Ashley do? According to the newspaper reports he has an affair and gets caught. Well, actually he has five affairs or one night stands, often with "glamour models" that he has picked up in a night club. No big deal you might think. It can happen to everyone.

But then there was the time when he was at the England World Cup base in South Africa and just a few hours before their first game he was sending sex texts to a model he had seen on the internet. He had never met this woman before and he was apparently begging her to send him "a really dirty" naked picture of herself. A few days later before the next game he was at it again. Altogether he sent 139 text messages in a month.

There is something about Premier League footballers and sex. They just can't get enough. John Terry, the ex-Chelsea and England defender, has made the headlines on a number of occasions with none more interesting than the time that he was caught having an extra-marital affair with the ex-girlfriend of his club and country teammate Wayne Bridge. Another big name caught with his shorts down was Wayne Rooney who allegedly had sex seven times with a prostitute while his wife, Coleen, was pregnant with their first child.

And let's not forget Ryan Giggs. The loyal Ryan Giggs who spent 29 years at Manchester United. The not so loyal Ryan Giggs who had an extra-marital affair with a former Miss Wales and *Big Brother* contestant. Bad enough you might think but this is also the same Ryan Giggs who had an eight year affair with his brother's wife and then had the nerve, like John Terry, to seek a super injunction to stop the media telling us about it.

It's not just their infidelity and seedy sex lives that I despise it's their almost insatiable greed. Let's look at Ashley Cole again. Just before he flew out to South Africa, he sent a text to some friends (amazing but he does have friends) saying "I hate England and the f***ing people." These were the people who were paying to see him every week so that he could pick up his £100,000 a week wage packet. Ashley wasn't always so well paid of course. There was a time when he was offered the paltry sum of £55,000 a week by Arsenal. He was reportedly trembling with anger as he sent a text saying that he was being "treated like a slave."

Greed is endemic among Premier League footballers. Take Raheem Sterling, an amazingly talented 20 year old. He had been nurtured and protected by Liverpool. He had been good for them but the club had been good for him. They had undoubtedly played a large part in making him the player that he was. And don't forget he was just 20 years old. So what did he do? He rejected a £35,000 a week pay rise which would have taken his earnings to £100,000 a week and moved to Manchester City. More recently Alexis Sanchez is reported to have told his club, Arsenal, that he wants £400,000 a week to stay with them. The greedy bastards.

Drug taking is another issue that some of these spoilt, super-rich egotists get involved in. Adrian Mutu received a seven month ban for taking cocaine while at Chelsea. The Manchester United defender Jaap Stam was banned for four months to having nandrolone in his system while just across the city Kolo Toure, of Manchester City suffered a six month ban for taking a banned substance. The drugs in this case were weight loss tablets which Toure said belonged to his wife and which he took "by mistake."

And let's not forget Rio Ferdinand. He had been told in advance that he was required to give a sample for drug testing when he was at Manchester United's training ground. Unfortunately he left without providing the sample, saying afterwards that he simply forgot. His failure to put a reminder on his expensive smart phone or even to make a note on a piece of paper cost him dear. He received an eight month ban and a £50,000 fine.

If you want a good insight into the Premier League, you could do worse than read *I Am The Secret Footballer: Lifting The Lid On The Beautiful Game*, published by Guardian Books. If you want to read about a $130,000 Las Vegas bar bill for one night out this is the book. Or what about the wife who came home, found her footballer husband in bed with another woman? You might expect her to throw a tantrum, shout, scream and tell him to leave by the nearest door. But no, she simply went out shopping, came back when hubby had finished and prepared a lovely meal for him as if nothing had happened. As the author says "They simply cannot do without a designer wardrobe, two weeks in Dubai and half of Tiffany's every Christmas and birthday, and so look the other way."

But I can forgive these obscenely rich young men their weakness for sex. Footballers are not the only people who commit adultery or go with prostitutes. And which hot-blooded male wouldn't find it hard to resist the advances of young beautiful women, willing to do anything for a night with a footballing celebrity. I can also forgive them their greed and bad taste. Wouldn't we all buy a garage full of cars, or bottles of champagne at £5,000 a pop if we earned £200,000 or more a week? You've got to spend it on something.

What I can't forgive them, however, is their behaviour on the pitch. I can't forgive them when they throw their hand in the air as soon as the ball goes out of play. They know it came off them and they know it's the other team's throw-in but they just have to try and con the referee. And I can't forgive them when they just have to gain that extra yard when they have a free kick. But worst of all I can't forgive them when they deliberately foul an opposing player when he's through on goal – the so-called *'professional foul'*. And I can't forgive them when they pull an opponent's shirt in the penalty area to stop him getting the ball and when they dive to the ground writhing in agony at the merest of touches, and often without being touched at all. They are cheats and they are dishonest. The most important thing to them is to win and to win at any cost.

All of this is against the rules and spirit of football. It's unsportsmanlike, it's ungentlemanly and it has no place in the wonderful game of football. Far be it from me to stereotype anyone but these arrogant, pampered, selfish young men, cocooned in their ridiculously squalid and wealthy world of sleaze fully deserve their place in their final team.

26   Southerners

Southerners, and by that I mean anyone born on or below a line between Bristol and London but excluding anyone from Devon and Cornwall (these westcountry weirdos are a race apart), are a pain in the bum. To a northerner a southerner is epitomised by London's Sloane Ranger set and by the Yuppies of Margaret Thatcher's 1980's Britain and it is these particular southerners that I hate the most. They are among the most detestable, good-for-nothing, supercilious, pompous asses that have ever walked upon the earth.

The age old saying that it's *soft down south* is so true and the people who live there are softer than cotton wool. The reason for this could well have something to do with work that southerners do. Up north they are grafters, they work long hours doing hard menial jobs whereas down south nobody gets their hands dirty; they all seem to work in marketing, PR, advertising or IT. There are no chimneys down south.

And then there's the weather which as you might expect is also soft. Up north they get real weather; rain, snow, winds and more rain. Down south it never rains. They suffer day after day of unbroken sunshine with not a cloud in the sky.

And if the wind blows it's a breeze so light that not even a blade of grass is disturbed. Down south it is always idyllically warm.

You wouldn't know that it's warm, of course. The mercury could be hitting the 30°C and the Met Office could be issuing warnings of sunstroke but on a Sunday afternoon the women will still be out at their garden parties dressed as though they were arctic explorers. And on the terraces at Stamford Bridge the men will be wearing five layers of clothes whilst stamping their feet to keep warm and singing some obscure ditty as the referee blows his whistle to stop the match every 15 minutes so that the players can take on life saving water. Everyone wears a coat down south.

No one is going to argue that southerners are anything but soft and perhaps it has something to do with the stuff they call food but which we call fancy, foreign muck. They eat some very strange stuff down south such as *empanadas* – organic veggie of course. And they insist on buying their bread from the farmers market or from some little known artisan baker down an alley just behind Borough Market.

Other favourites apparently are purple asparagus and seaweed popcorn. Yes, they both taste and look as bad as they sound. And did you know that octopus is the new squid and fruit flavoured water is the new soda. Of course you did. And who but a southerner would drink *bacon flavoured bourbon*.

The main problem with southerners, from a northern perspective, is that they are lazy, stuck-up, pretentious wankers. Most of them work in the city doing deals and they would think nothing of ripping off their old granny if it meant that they could make another grand or two.

They are all upper middle class (or think they are) so they vote Green or Liberal f***ing Democrat and go to pamper days at some exclusive spa or wellness centre and then to an exclusive nightclub such as Boujis or Annabel's where they pay mega bucks for a small glass of champagne and play spot the northerner. He's the one leaning on the bar, looking lost and gripping his bottle of Belgian wheat beer (he's drinking this only because this poncey southern bar doesn't sell his beloved Boddys or indeed any draught beer) with both hands just in case he loses it which he thinks would be a disaster of Titanic proportions - which it would be, of course, at the f***ing price that he paid for it. Southerners are always whinging about northerners; usually about how poor they are. They have a chip on their shoulder bigger than the London Shard.

The other thing that I hate about southerners is that they are so bloody unfriendly. They would never talk to a complete stranger. They only speak to what they call the chavs (that is anyone who does any real work such as everyone working in a shop, all tradesmen and the person delivering their weekly groceries) because they feel that they have to. They rarely even talk to their own kind but when they do, their highly intellectual conversation usually concerns house prices, their villa in Tuscany or how lazy northerners are.

Annoyingly if a southerner is on public transport (and this only ever happens in London) he will never offer his seat up to an older person or to someone who is pregnant. Why should he? It's not his fault that they are old or couldn't keep their legs together.

And of course, they speak a foreign language, if language is what it is. It is certainly not the Queen's English. This is true across the whole of the south but never more so than in and around the Capital where yes is pronounced *yah*, and *rairly* is their speak for really.

Elsewhere this wonderful argot uses *jollop* for going out and having a good time, *squippy* for hyperactive and *dorleybowl* for a bad haircut. If you ever have the misfortune to find yourself down south and someone approaches you and says *hello sweetiedarls* don't whatever you do be offended. All they are saying is 'how are you and what's the gossip!' And should you be trying to get into some trendy club in Belgravia (though God knows why you would want to) and someone says *Sorry dahling it's GLO* don't argue, just walk away and pity the poor bastards. GLO is their way of keeping the ordinary person out. GLO is guest list only.

To a southerner everything is described as either *frightfully* or *ghastly*. For example a typical southern conversation might be *Dahling, the weather at Klosters was just ghastly this year and we bumped into that frightfully boring man Nigel.* It makes me want to spit.

Personally I think that the government should relocate all southerners to Bath, Cheltenham, or Henley or some other such hoity-toity southern enclave and let them get on with their own pathetic miserable lives in their very own exclusive club. If that's not going to happen then the minimum they should do should be to provide anyone who strays over the border from the north with counselling and first class accompanied transportation home.

I am not sure whether it is official or government policy but southerners also have a different currency to the rest of the country with one southern pound being equal to around 33 pence. This means that everything down south is bloody expensive. A southerner can go out on a Saturday night, have two or three raspberry flavoured sour craft beers and maybe one champagne cocktail and a line of coke and when he wakes in the morning with a head that feels as if it is being gnawed at by some as yet to be discovered reptile he'll check his smartphone App just to confirm that he had spent £25 short of a thousand pounds.

And did I mention that southerners like a drink? It's a well-known fact that 90% of England's alcoholics are southerners. To be honest on this issue I do have some sympathy with them. If I had to live in some prissy contemptible place surrounded by egotistical halfwits where the most popular cultural pursuit was choosing between a cappuccino and a macchiato, I would be pissed out of my head every single minute of every single day.

There is, then, a lot to dislike southerners for but what swings it for me is the fact that if you meet a southerner up north he will always be telling you how wonderful it is back home. "Down south even the corner shop stocks matsutake mushrooms, we have better public transport, the beer's cheaper, people are not so nosy and I have a choice of private doctors and hospitals" they'll say. By now you will know what my response is. FOBTT. If it's so bloody good down south and so bloody bad up here then piss off. For that reason alone southerners will be dispatched to the Island. At least they won't have far to go.

27   Slim women

Everyone loves a slim woman, or do they? No they most certainly do not. Mrs Scady and her lady friends absolutely detest them. They bitch about them constantly as only women of a certain age and build do. And the worst ones, the super slim women, come in for the most vicious of their rants at their weekly get together in our local Tea Shoppe where they sip Earl Grey tea in china cups and munch their way through a plate full of hot buttered tea cakes.

These are the women with a waist the size of one of Mrs Scady's arms. She hates them with a passion. In her eyes any female of a size fourteen or under should be force fed avocados, nuts, deep fried haloumi cheese and crisps by the bucketful. This is, of course, very similar to Mrs Scady's own diet. These poor unfortunates would then be forced to spend the rest of their lives in garments of at least a size twenty. Coincidentally Mrs Scady has several wardrobes full of such items which she has discarded because they are a little 'tight' on her. She claims they must have shrunk in the wash. Slim women make Mrs Scady sick, but not sick enough to lose weight.

Every now and again I go shopping with Mrs Scady and it's here, in the clothes shop that these creatures come into their own. You can hear them agonising over whether it's to be a size six or size eight whilst Mrs Scady is looking for a tent to cover up her cellulite and bingo wings. Apparently it is even worse when they get into the changing rooms. They are there showing off their scanty thong and their perfectly erect nipples whilst Mrs Scady is doing her best not to show anyone her greying full cup bosom armoury and plentiful sagging bottom. "Oooooh, this is so baggy" says the slim young thing in her size six whilst Mrs Scady struggles to force up the zip and stuff her fat rolls into her size sixteen.

Mrs Scady finds this utterly depressing and inevitably, after one of these forays we always end up in the Cornish pasty shop for comfort food.

Over the years Mrs Scady and I have been to numerous office parties where the slim girls are flaunting their gorgeously spray tanned 'skin and bone' in the direction of their naive little male admirers. They teeter around on their heels, flashing their whitened teeth as they concentrate their whole attention on looking sumptuously thin. It is pathetic and it shows no understanding of, or sympathy for, the larger ladies present in their size sixteen party frock and sensible shoes. They are invisible.

As a man I accept some blame for this. In every other area of life we want 'more' but in women we want 'less'.

Mrs Scady's daughter is slim (she obviously inherited her father's genes) and when the three of us go out for a meal it can be very painful. Firstly the waiter brings the menus and hands them to the daughter completely blanking Mrs Scady, the fat girl. I get some attention because as the solitary male it is assumed that I am paying. Next we have the agony of the daughter pouring over the menu and working out which dish has the least calories.

Mrs Scady chooses the pasta with a creamy sauce with some garlic bread whilst her daughter chooses the grilled hake with rocket garnish. Mrs Scady and I have a full bodied red wine whilst the daughter has the dry white, of course. Half way through her measly piece of fish she announces that she couldn't eat another thing and that her trousers are just sooooo tight. 'Oh look at my stomach' she says as she puts her knife and fork in the finished position. On one occasion Mrs Scady mentioned that she was feeling a bit fat too after her meal and her daughter replied 'Oh you're not as fat as me' at which point I had to physically restrain Mrs Scady.

The beach is of course the place where a slim woman steals the show and has the admiration of not just her boyfriend but everyone else's boyfriend, other people's husbands and every waiter in sight. She runs daintily into the sea with not a ripple of fat to be seen and barely makes a splash as her body hits the water. The whole beach watches her cavorting with her boyfriend and they're all wondering if they're having sex below the water line. The beach is full of cleverly concealed erections and women whose eyes reveal envy and hatred. The bikini-clad nymph then emerges from the sea with a Mona Lisa smile on her face and droplets of water glistening on her perfectly toned skin, whilst other, shall I say, larger women emerge like a beached whale with half of their bottom and one of their breasts hanging out of their Marks and Spencer swimsuit. Life can be very unfair.

Personally I do not dislike a woman for being slim but I am becoming increasingly angry at their misguided views on size and at their obsessive adherence to the sordid goal of 'thin'. They are vainglorious, shallow human beings and as such they have outstayed their presence among normal society. They will be going.

28   Drinkers

This was difficult. Like most people I like a couple of glasses of wine with my meal on a Saturday night and the odd pint or two of real ale down at my local pub. I do not consider this to be excessive and I certainly do not see this as cause for me and others of my ilk to be deported to some God forsaken island. I am a drinker but there are drinkers and there are *drinkers* and so for the sake of clarity and to avoid the possibility of the wrong people being shot it is this last category that will be going to the free bar in the sky.

The drinker is someone who is addicted to alcohol and who cannot have just one glass. I have known many of these people. They are obsessed by pubs, and whilst they wouldn't be able to find the village library they can sniff out a pub from a mile away. You've heard of Pooh bear and the honey? That's a drinker, but their particular nectar is alcohol and their favourite people are those who want to join them on their drunken rollercoaster ride.

I have a friend called Paul who is a drinker. When he met his first wife he asked her if she 'liked a drink'. The alarm bells should have started ringing right away but it took her about four months to realise that, if she stayed with him, it was going to be a marriage of many different personas, including the occasionally sober one. Princess Diana thought that she had problems when there were 'three in this marriage'; she should have been grateful for only three. When you live with a drinker you never quite know who's going to show up, but you get to know most of the characters quite well.

Much depended upon whether Paul was drinking wine or beer; each had a different effect but the end result was usually the same. Beer was usually drunk in a pub; his first pint giving him an attractive glow; he smiled more readily and became beautifully relaxed. His wife loved him when he had one pint. The second pint saw him become slightly red in the face and then very chatty and happy with a propensity to buy drinks for everyone. I loved him at this stage. Everybody loved him. There was a lot of football chat and he sometimes even told his wife that she was attractive; she knew this was a lie, but she swallowed it. At this stage things were still pleasant and under control. The third pint was the beginning of the slippery slope; he would leer at young women, talk too loudly and interrupt others when they were talking. She sometimes tried to reign him in at this point but it usually evoked a 'where's your sense of humour?' line.

It's on the fourth pint that he started to tell his stories of when he fought in the Vietnam War (which occurred when he was still in short trousers). Women who are not very well orientated in time swallowed the whole story and he would always offer to show them his war wounds. Pint numbers five and six saw him moving into the poo phase. He would recount stories of when he and a friend were on their way home from the pub and his bowels suddenly exploded, or about his time with the Royal Marines in Plymouth and the ritual *dance of the burning bum.* Apparently on a night out drinking there would always be one particularly drunken Marine who would dance on the table stark bollock naked with a flaming rolled up newspaper up his ass. Before the flames reached his skin the fire would be extinguished by his other buddies throwing their pints over him. I bet the pub landlord was pleased.

It was at this stage that Paul would graphically describe the poo running down his legs and how his friend heroically took off his tee-shirt to clean him up; at this point he is laughing uncontrollably and letting slip the odd fart. The women who were previously enthralled tended to distance themselves at this point.

There was a slight difference when he drank wine because the mellow phase lasted a bit longer and there was even a pleasant lull before the storm after which he progressed towards 'very loud' and totally overpowering.

When a group of drinkers get together over a meal there are two pre-requisites: plenty of wine and someone willing to pour it freely and generously; Paul was, of course, the perfect host in this respect. He and his wife often had a family dinner and it invariably ended in tears because of alcohol. She was usually accused of lacking humour as her son, daughter and husband opened the fourth bottle. Her son would get on his political high horse and Paul would egg him on and up the volume with his intellectual and opinionated rants. Their daughter meanwhile was quiet and just poured herself another glass and then another one and then another one.

Wine and weddings go well together and the drinker is always happy to receive a wedding invitation provided it isn't from a Mormon or a Muslim. On these occasions the wine tends to flow freely and drinkers always make sure that they are seated between two non-drinkers; this means that there is more of the stuff for them.

At weddings drinkers always laugh more loudly than anyone else at the jokes that aren't at all funny and shout out highly inappropriate remarks during the speeches.

Once the bride and groom have cut the cake and been up for the first dance, it's the drinker that is next on the dance floor, either alone or with anyone fool enough to dance with him. This would usually be small children, much to the horror of their parents. The drinker thinks that he is a good dancer and the more he has to drink the more that this misguided idiot performs his moves as he monopolises the whole dance floor. Embarrassing does not really do it justice. Mrs Scady's daughter has yet to get married and has made her mum promise that my friend, Paul, will not be invited to the wedding let alone allowed on the dance floor.

As anyone who knows me will testify I am not one to find fault in people or criticise their activities but drinkers are obnoxious, self-indulgent, overbearing and unpleasant. They care not one jot for others who might be around them because the universe is centred on them. They are grotesque, thoughtless and selfish and they have outstayed their welcome – the bar is closed.

29   The Welsh

At the age of 90 my mum was still going on holidays with her gang of friends, all of a similar age. One of her favourite places was Minehead on the north coast of Somerset. After one such visit I remember asking her, like the dutiful son, if she had enjoyed her holiday. "Yes, thanks," she said, and then after a slight hesitation "Full of Welsh people." And then, perhaps a minute later, she added "Funny buggers the Welsh."

And "funny buggers" they most certainly are. Why for a start do they have two national emblems – the leek and the daffodil? The daffodil I can understand. If you have ever seen a field of daffodils you will know just how beautiful they are. Ask Wordsworth. But a leek? A vegetable? They may as well have chosen a carrot or a turnip, or if they wanted something exotic how about a courgette? They would all be equally stupid. No one chooses a vegetable as an emblem of their country – except the Welsh.

One of the biggest problems with the Welsh, of course, is that you can never understand what they are saying. They have their own language which is totally incomprehensible to 99.9999% of the world's population. It's not really a language; it's a made up way of confusing people into believing that there is such a thing as a Welsh language.

There isn't. It's a con and if you think I am being a little harsh, have a go at pronouncing this word Llanfairpwllgwyngyllgogerychwyrndrobwllllantysiliogogogoch". See what I mean. This is the name of a small village on the island of Anglesey and according to Wikipedia it means "St Mary's church in the hollow of the white hazel near to the fierce whirlpool of St Tysilio of the red cave". What rubbish. Let's be honest it's really a load of letters put together in a totally random order to fool the rest of us. They will tell you, again particularly if you are English, that their language is a part of the great Welsh culture, this being something that the English do not have. As with everything else that they say this is a load of rubbish. Nowhere is the Welsh culture more evident than in the annual National Eisteddfod.

They will tell you that this is an ancient national celebration of Welsh culture with poetry, dance, literature and music – all in the Welsh language. What it really is though is an excuse for hundreds of strange Welsh men and women to gather in a field in the middle of nowhere, dressed in what looks very similar to a white bedsheet while dancing around in circles babbling in an incoherent language before eventually going home to their humdrum lives in the valleys. This supposed "ancient" festival was first held in the mid 19th century – old maybe but hardly ancient.

The Welsh are an annoying race and one of the most annoying things they do is to sing. Give a Welshman any excuse and he will burst into song; get two or more of them together and they form a choir. There are few things more annoying in this world than a Welsh male voice choir in full flow. I know that they have boring lives, I can appreciate the suffering they must go through on a daily basis just having to live in Wales but surely there is a better way to ease the pain. Couldn't they just go to the pub and get pissed like a normal person? Couldn't they take up stamp collecting or trainspotting instead? Don't get me wrong, I have no problem with Tom Jones or Charlotte Church, it's just the rest of them and I wish they would just shut up.

Up until now I have not mentioned the biggest problem with the Welsh. Ask any Englishman about the Welsh and it's a certainty that you will be told that they have a close relationship with sheep. They (or more accurately the men in Wales) are, to put it bluntly, sheep shaggers. I have no idea if this is true but I have always thought that there is "no smoke without fire" and so there must be a degree of truth in this long held view. So what, you might ask. Does it matter as long as both parties are consenting?

It goes without saying that the Welsh hate the English or that's what they say. Hate in this instance is another word for envy. The Welsh are jealous of the English and of everything that England has achieved, and nowhere is this truer than in sport. The Welsh believe that they are world-beaters at rugby. When they win a match, particularly if it's against England, they truly believe that they are rulers of the world. In their sad and woebegone eyes there is no greater achievement but what they tend to always forget is that we, the English, have won a few more matches than they have. Of the 129 matches played Wales have won 57 and England 60. The Welsh also forget the tremendous victory by England in 2003 when we lifted the Rugby World Cup in Australia. No surprise of course when the best they have ever achieved is third place back in 1987.

And what about football? In this king of all sports the two countries have played each other 92 times, with England winning 67 of these encounters and the Welsh just 14. Total dominance by England. I won't even mention cricket.

The Welsh are always moaning. They moan about the English (of course) and they moan about being a part of the UK but when they get a chance to leave they vote to stay. They go on about the weather – it's always raining – and they moan about the lack of jobs. They blame everyone else for the decline of their traditional industries, whilst choosing to ignore the billions of pounds that have been invested there. They are a nation of whingers and that is not just my opinion. It's official. A survey reported on Wales Online concluded that the inhabitants of Cardiff are the biggest moaners in Britain. Wales Online agreed saying that there was clear evidence to show that Cardiff was the "UK's whining capital".

And finally, why is it that 99% of Welsh people have the same name. They are either called Jones, Evans or Williams? To be honest this is irrelevant. It doesn't matter what they are called or why. They are included. They will be in the queue. They have earned their place as those chosen to spend the rest of their days on the IOW.

30   White Van Man

We have all met them or should I say we have all seen them – White Van Man (WMV). You look up and there they are. A second ago they were nowhere in sight and yet there they are filling your rear view mirror, waving as if their life depended on it for you to move over. You check your speed and as you thought you are doing just under 90 mph in the fast lane of the motorway and yet they look at you as though you're a Sunday afternoon driver out for a quiet drive in the country.

Flash, flash. They are now inches from the back of your car. What do you do? Slow down just to annoy him; too dangerous. You know that they only have half a brain cell at best which means that their reaction time will be slow. So slow that they will inevitably just drive into the back of you. Speed up? No, that's not an option either. You are already well over the speed limit and you think you are going fast enough anyway. Flash, flash. Their waving is even more frantic and you can see WVM mouthing some obscenity at you while slowly making a hand gesture which even your four year old son knows the meaning of. He is suggesting that you are the wanker! What irony. You want to kill him but you give in and move over.

He overtakes and pulls in immediately in front of you so close that you have to push your foot down on the brake and pray. And then he disappears off into the distance to surprise some other unsuspecting soul. Bastard!

Along with BMW drivers the drivers of white vans are, without a doubt, the most detested people on the road. The Urban Dictionary defines WVM as a threat to road safety and states that he drives as though he is on a fairground dodgem. Most of them, it says, have an IQ lower than their shoe size. Personally I think this last one is a bit generous but other than that it's spot on.

What is it about a white van that turns an ordinary person into a pasty eating, mobile phone using, foul-mouthed imbecile? Or were they like that before they opened the van door? What came first the chicken or the egg? I know where my money is. I've driven a white van before as have many of my friends (not as a job or hobby you understand but a van hired when I've needed to move furniture) and I've not turned into a cross between a two-headed Neanderthal on speed and an escapee from a high security mental institution.

There are apparently 2.5 million white vans on the road and the number is growing every year with the popularity of internet shopping and the need for even more delivery drivers. Strangely they are not all white of course. These boy racers will drive any colour van but it's the white variety that seems to bring out the worst in them.

It's not just delivery drivers. The biggest culprits are the self-employed cowboys otherwise known as plumbers, electricians and builders. For some inexplicable reason they all think that they are Formula 1 drivers behind the wheel of a V8, 32 valve, turbo-charged racing car on the final lap of the Monaco grand prix. All they have to do is pass the car in front (you!), receive the chequered flag, open the bubbly and spend the evening in the casino with a bevy of scantily clad blondes on their arm and later in their bed. Dream on.

The reality, of course, is that the vehicle they are driving is a clapped out, rust-bucket, they are on their way from one job to another (to rip off some old lady by charging her five times what the job really costs) and they live in Chingford or Gravesend – or some other similar hell-hole. They will almost certainly regularly stop at Clacket Lane services, the murder capital of the M25.

The term WVM was reportedly first used by Sarah Kennedy on a BBC Radio 2 programme in 1997. It resonated so much with the general public that it was not long before it became a part of daily use. Its popularity as a description for bad drivers was instant because we all recognised WVM. We had all experienced WVM and knew what the expression stood for. The Cambridge Dictionary describes this as a derogatory term, with the WVM being:

"A man who is thought to be typical of drivers of white vans by being rude, not well educated, and having very strong, often unpleasant opinions."

But is all this true? Is the typical WVM an aggressive tattooed lager swilling 22 year old lout; someone who lives on junk food, spends his weekends in the pub or at a football match and invariably owns a Rottweiler. Or is this simply a nasty stereotype dreamed up by a middle class PR executive; a myth perpetuated by the media because it suits them to have something by which they can keep the working class in their place.

You will not be surprised to know that WVM has been the subject of numerous surveys and academic studies. One such study carried out by the Social Issues Research Centre showed that the average age of WVM is 37 with the majority of drivers being in their 30's or 40's. He, and invariably it is a he, with women making up just 4% of all white van drivers, will probably be married. And although the majority will be listening to a local radio station as they ply their way on the country's roads, many are just as likely to be listening to tapes of opera or Classic FM. As you might expect WVM drives a lot of miles each year but surprisingly nearly 70% of them have made no insurance claims.

So are we being unfair. Are they really merely misunderstood? Are we maligning them as devils when really they are saints? Possibly, if this headline from the Manchester Evening News is typical: "Heroic white van men rescue three people from burning Stockport house – then continue on to work." The two white van men had stopped at some traffic lights and saw two men and a woman hanging out of an upstairs window shouting for help – the house obviously on fire. Without thinking they reversed their van 50 yards up the drive of the house to a point just under the window so that the occupants of the house could drop onto the roof of the van and safety. The white van men then drove off to work – because they were late!

And then there was the case of a 63 year old lady driver from Kent who had an accident at a busy junction. She was shaken and the car was stuck half on the kerb and half on the road. Motorists just drove by shouting abuse at her for blocking their way but then came WVM. She steadied herself for more abuse but very much against the stereotype he stopped his vehicle, put on a hi-vis jacket, and started to divert the traffic.

The problem is that for every good news story there are a 100 horrific ones. Having studied the WMV subject extensively I will be the first to admit that not all white van drivers are the same and that there are undoubtedly some who are careful, considerate and who visit their granny every week. On balance, however, there are far too many white van drivers who perfectly fit the WMV stereotype - of the van driver who is forever changing lanes, sees no need to indicate, thinks tailgating is an acceptable way of driving, and is aggressive and abusive to all other road users. They, therefore, thoroughly deserve their place on the ferry.

31   Caravan owners

After following the bloody thing for 14 miles who hasn't raged and screamed at the caravan in front? BMW drivers are hated, white van man is despised and cyclists are detested but it's the obnoxious dickhead towing a caravan that is, arguably, the most loathed person on the road. And rightly so.

You have to be a certain sort of person to want to tow a caravan behind you. And that sort of person is stark staring bonkers. You have to be a certain sort of person to leave your comfortable home and spend your holidays in a tin box and that sort of person is an idiot. A caravan owner is the sort of person that thinks walking to the local shop to buy a newspaper is an adventure. But then again, for them I guess it is. Because their idea of fun is to imitate a snail by dragging an aluminium shell on wheels hundreds of miles at a maximum speed of 40 miles per hour whilst behind them is an ever increasing trail of angry, motorists.

And when they get to wherever they are going what do they do? I'll tell you. Absolutely nothing. He will sit and read his newspaper – inside the caravan if it's raining, windy, snowing or in any other way too bloody bad to venture out, and outside on the 5% of days when the sun is shining and the temperature reaches the heady heights of 18°c. She will be inside cooking up a heart-attack inducing fry-up.

Getting stuck behind a caravan is hell. You can't get too close because they are yawing from side to side like a sidewinder snake in the Mojave Desert; so much that you are convinced that they are going to topple over, which unfortunately happens all too infrequently. This makes overtaking much more difficult especially on narrower roads. And, of course, they are so damn big that you can't see around them. So you are stuck and as every mile slowly grinds on your impatience level increases disproportionately until you break; you can't take it anymore.

You pull out to overtake only to be confronted by a huge truck heading straight towards you. You're on the wrong side of the road, about to be obliterated and it's all the fault of the selfish tosspot in the 'van'.

Caravan owners generally fall into two distinct categories. Both are equally bad and they will be led out to meet their fate together. First there is what are called the *Grey Nomads*. These are the people who have spent all their working lives saving up for and dreaming of retirement and of how they will then be able to go anywhere they like with their caravan. They are always grey haired, short (under 5 foot 3 inches), often hunched-back and inevitably he will be wearing a cloth cap and a cardigan and she will be dressed in her Sunday best (she always is no matter what the day is). Both will be sporting those detestable flip up sunglasses. These are the people who spend up to six weeks at a time hauling their home-from-home around with them from one dreary and depressing caravan park to another.

The second group are the LCAWUC's or the lower class alcoholics with unruly children. They may only be holidaying for a week, because that's all they can afford but their impact on the rest of us is no less for that. The odds are that you will bump into these annoying people at some roadside services. You'll hear them first. He'll be shouting at the children as they run amok in the shop clamouring for yet another packet of tooth-rotting sugar sweets and she'll be shouting at him because he's shouting at her darling little kids. They will, of course, be stocking up on crisps, chocolate and cheap, strong own-label brand cider. They know how to live.

I can just about understand why people might want to spend a holiday in a caravan in a field full of cowpats in

Cornwall with the rain drilling into the roof like bullets from an AK-47 hitting corrugated iron. Good luck to them. Let them do it I say. If they are there they won't be bothering me when I'm swimming up to the pool bar for my third sex-on-the-beach as the sun relentlessly shines in the Dom Rep. If they prefer their particular version of heaven they can have it. They can drive themselves to a holiday park and rent a static caravan. It's easy. There is absolutely no need, however, for them or anyone else to tow a caravan and it should be banned. It's anti-social behaviour on a par with letting your dog crap on a playing field or playing (c)rap music in public. I suspect that the first political party to include a total ban on caravans in their manifesto will get the biggest majority of any party ever.

My hatred of caravans and thus of their owners is without boundaries. I loathe and detest them with a passion and if I could I would ban them from the roads, crush them and banish their owners to secure institutions. Once there I would subject these poor unfortunate souls to whatever treatment was available – drugs, electric shocks and as a last resort trepanning – until they admitted to the error of their ways and begged for forgiveness and to be accepted back into society. They are bad people and they have earned their place against on the Island.

32   Daily Mail readers

A post by La Boheme on the Digital Spy online forum describes a typical Daily Mail reader as someone *'who espouses the paper's right-wing, middle-England, anti-immigrant, racist, misogynist, homophobic, anti-intellectual, sanctimonious mind-set'.* Wow! Do you think that La Boheme is a lefty, Guardian reading ex hippy-chick or an aspiring upper middle-class, Telegraph reading blue-rinse Tory from the Shires? One or the other surely but whoever she is I agree wholeheartedly with her portrayal of these worthless turds. If I am in one of my rare generous moods I like to think of Daily Mail readers as foolish, people who are easily deceived and who should be pitied and helped. . At other times I see them for the brainless, intolerant, jaundiced, self-righteous, self-engrossed, deviants that they are.

I like to think that there are newspaper owners, editors and journalists out there who have a passion for what they do, that they acknowledge the power of the fourth estate and the responsibility that this brings. I like to believe that there are newspaper proprietors and editors out there who are more concerned about what is written in their newspaper and how it is written than they are with advertising revenue and sales figures. And I dream that there are journalists working who want to report the facts rather than sensationalise and that there are editors who insist that a story is investigated and verified before it is printed.

I'm sure that all of these people exist but if they do they are certainly not working on the Daily Mail. This is, without a shred of doubt, an abomination of a newspaper. Its ethos, if it can be said to have one, is to exaggerate and sensationalise everything, with nothing being more important than the next headline. The Daily Mail is an obscene publication and everyone involved in its production should be ashamed of themselves. They won't be of course because these despicable creatures work to a different set of values to you and me. They care not a jot for what is right or wrong so long as their sales and readership figures continue to grow. This is a *rag*, par excellence.

All journalists know that a good headline is crucially important. Without it even the best of stories will go unread. The Daily Mail has taken the art of headline writing to a completely new level with each one becoming more ridiculous than the previous one.

There is no doubt that they achieve their job, they grab your attention and they make you want to read the story even if it is for no other reason than to find out what the hell it is all about. A simple glance at some Daily Mail headlines demonstrates just how unbelievably farcical they are:

How a romantic candle-lit dinner can give you cancer

Woman, 63, 'becomes PREGNANT in the mouth' with baby squid after eating calamari

How using Facebook could raise your risk of cancer

Food watchdog warning over peanut butter brand containing 'cancer-causing fungus'

Big headed babies 'more prone to cancer'

What is it about the Daily mail and its pathological obsession with cancer?

They say that a picture is worth a thousand words and this is a maxim that the Daily Mail has embraced wholeheartedly. Unfortunately the pictures chosen to illustrate a story all too often have little or nothing to do with the actual story itself. The pictures used will almost always be of a woman and will concentrate on either the subject's boobs or legs. In April 2017 the Daily Mail reported on the meeting of the British Prime Minister, Theresa May and Scotland's First Minister, Nicola

Sturgeon. The meeting was billed elsewhere as being a crucial part of the discussions on how England and Scotland would work together after the UK's exit from the EU. But how did the Daily Mail report this important occasion? By showing a picture of both politician's legs under the headline "Never mind Brexit, who won Legs-it?"

Previously the Daily Mail reported on an international conference held in London to discuss sexual violence by publishing a picture of Amal Alamuddin, a respected barrister specialising in international law and human rights. The Mail's caption to the picture was 'George Clooney's fiancée Amal Alamuddin looks stylish in striking red dress and fetching floral heels at sexual violence summit'. Unbelievable but true.

Bad though they undoubtedly are, it is not the Daily Mail's owners who will be first against the wall. It's not even the so-called journalists who pen the trash that the paper publishes.

The people who I despise the most and the people who will be marched on to the boats for the short journey across the water are the people who read the bloody thing. In terms of circulation the Daily Mail is the second most popular newspaper in the country; each day it is bought by nearly 1.5 million people. Each and every one of them is guilty. Without its readers the Daily Mail would not exist and it is for this crime that they will find themselves standing shoulder to shoulder with many of the people that they themselves hate.

33   Born Again Christians

How, you might ask, can I possibly include someone who believes in God in a list of those that are going to be marched out at dawn, put on a ferry and deported to the God-damned Isle of Wight?   What have they possibly done to deserve such a terrible fate, I hear you ask. Actually this was an easy decision; there was no debate, no consideration and there are no regrets. You might think that being a Christian means that you are kind, forgiving, altruistic, selfless, peaceful, humble, respectful and compassionate. You would be wrong. These are Christian values for sure but simply saying that you accept Christ as Saviour or believe in God does not mean that these can be automatically applied to you. The vast majority of the so-called 'believers' that I have met have been some of the most mean-spirited, miserable, spiteful people that I have ever met. And the very worst of them have been the Born Again Christians. Read on.

According to Born Again Christian beliefs, all men (and presumably women) are sinners. We are born sinners and no matter what we do to try to be a good person we will remain a sinner unless we become *born again*. A multi-millionaire can give all of his money away to charity but he will still be a sinner. You or I could spend our lives working with homeless people, or in a hospice, or doing any amount of good work but none of this would stop us being sinners. You remain a sinner until you repent your sins and become born again and if you do not repent of your sins you will not go to Heaven. Who says so? Well, the Born Again Christians say so. And they also say that there is only one way into Heaven and that's to invite Christ into your life but you have to do it their way. You have to become one of them.

To get through those pearly gates all anyone has to do is acknowledge that they are a sinner and to accept that only Jesus can make them pure, i.e. not a sinner. They say that you should not just take their word for it and that you should check out the Bible. The Gospel of John, chapter 3 verses 3-5 to be precise in which Jesus is quoted as saying that "Very truly I tell you, no one can see the kingdom of God unless they are born again." And to be born again all you have to do is repent your sins. To do this you must go to church, sing hymns, pray, read the Bible and generally boast about how you believe in God.

It doesn't matter who you are – anyone can be born again. It doesn't matter what else you do – the odd bit of theft or even something bigger like killing someone. As long as you continue to say that you believe in God and repent and that you accept Christ as your Saviour, then you will be saved.

I have never heard such a load of utter rubbish in my life. If there is a God would he really deny a place in Heaven to someone who has dedicated their life to working for others or to someone who gave their millions towards the production of life-saving drugs, or to the person who threw their last pennies in a beggar's hat? Would God be so mean spirited to these people that he would say sorry, you didn't invite my son into your life, you didn't go to church, you didn't pray, so go away. You're a sinner. I sincerely hope not. I think not.

If there is a God surely he can see through all of the crap that the so-called believers amongst us put out. Surely God knows when someone is doing good or bad or when someone has goodness or evil in their heart and surely he is not so stupid as to be conned by the Born Again Christians into thinking that all anyone has to do, to be admitted into Heaven, is to go to church and repent your sins. Again, I think that God is better than this. I do not, for one moment, think that he is stupid. Far from it I would have thought. My guess is that he's looking down on the Born Again Brigade with a mischievous look on his wizened old face and thinking what a load of sanctimonious old tossers they are. Without a doubt he has his own plans for them but I can't for one minute believe that it's what they are expecting. It might begin with an H but it's sure as Hell not going to be Heaven.

There's a widely held view that there is nothing worse than a reformed "sinner"; the ex-smoker or drinker who preaches on and on about the dangers of cigarettes and alcohol, and heaps damnation on those who partake in either practice, whilst conveniently forgetting that they once were also addicted. Born Again Christians are the worst of these reformed "sinners".

They need to be born again because at some earlier stage in their life they were bad boys or girls but one day they became worried shitless that their past misdemeanours would result in them being sent down to stoke the fires of hell. And so they promise loudly and publicly to God that they will give their soul to Jesus, whilst muttering under their breath that it's in return for their place in Heaven.

Born Again Christians have a level of arrogance that is absolutely astounding. There they are looking down their noses at the rest of us because we are not one of them. They don't even know us. They certainly do not know what we think or what our beliefs are or what we do. All they see is that we are not with them in church and that we are not telling everyone that, like them, we believe in God (even if we do). It's unbelievable.

Just like the Jehovah's Witnesses they think that their way is the only correct way. They despise other religions and they believe that they are superior. And just like Jehovah's Witnesses they believe in the literal word of the Bible, or more accurately their particular interpretation of the Bible. They are ideological bigots and the way in which they adhere to their beliefs is more akin to the followers of some sinister cult than it is to a religion in which the fundamental tenets are forgiveness and understanding (particularly of people's failings). Born again Christians are about as un-Christian-like as it's possible to be.

Come the day, they will be there. No doubt that as they stare at the Island as it appears out of the mist they will continue to believe that they are on their way to a better place. Let them think it – the fools.

34   Morris Dancers

The UK has some great traditions. We are a culturally rich nation with a history and heritage of unsurpassed diversity. We are renowned as a country of eccentricity, full of folklore and myths and from Land's End to John O'Groats we proudly celebrate our local customs with a determination that stems from centuries of these weird and wonderful traditions being assimilated into our culture.

Take the annual cheese rolling event in Gloucester where people from all over the world now come to chase a round of Double Gloucester cheese down Cooper's Hill. Sounds ridiculous and it is. Chasing a cheese down a hill just for the hell of it is about as stupid as it gets but somehow it feels right. It feels British. And what about those mad men from Ottery St Mary in Devon who, every 5th of November, carry flaming tar barrels on their backs through the streets of the town for a reason or cause that was long ago forgotten. There is no sense in this at all but yet again it's a quintessentially British tradition that characterises everything that is good about this country.

And then there are Morris dancers. These people are stark staring bonkers. On any scale of lunatic eccentrics they are off it – by miles. Morris dancing is the complete opposite of cheese chasing or burning barrel carrying and Morris dancers epitomise everything that is wrong about this country. There was never a moment of doubt that they would be included here in this book. I didn't have to consider it for a millisecond, not a nanosecond, not even a unit of Planck time which is, I am told, the smallest amount of time that there can ever be. And if I ever gave Morris dancers or Morris dancing a Planck time of thought again it would be too much.

Morris dancing is just an excuse for totally inadequate bearded men and the occasional woman to dress up in rags, sew bells on their trousers, put on a stupid hat covered with foliage and flowers and bang a few sticks together while jumping up and down and shouting a few incomprehensible and utterly meaningless words.

To call what these people do a dance is generous in the extreme. It's not a dance. It can best be described as a group of men and women each of whom is jerking their arms and legs in a multitude of directions as if in some involuntary death-bed spasm. They are not in sync with each other and they are certainly not in time with the noise coming from the wizened old scrote playing the squeezebox.

Morris dancers are the worst dancers in the world, worse even than drunken dads at weddings. If you don't believe me have a careful look the next time you come across a gang of these weirdos in full flow. Look at them but also take a minute to study the other poor souls who, like you, are the audience. You'll see a look of bewilderment take over their face as they are immediately unsure of what they are witnessing. After bewilderment comes terror and their faces take on a rictus grin. This is when they start looking for the nearest exit, convinced that the mad men in front of them are about to attack at any second. You will see people back themselves up against the nearest wall or cower in groups as an automatic defence mechanism. Young children will scream and dogs will howl.

When it's all over and the barmy bell ringers have packed their clubs away and have moved on to the next unsuspecting victims the audience remain in a stupor. In time they recover of course but sub-consciously they have expunged what they have seen from their memories. They have to because it's the only way that they can ever sleep again.

Morris dancers are society's outcasts. They are nerds of the highest order. If they were to carry out their little rituals behind closed and locked doors there would be no problem. No normal human being would ever want to be a Morris dancer but if that is what they *need* to do then I could probably just about accept it. The big problem is that they do not do this thing in private. They insist on making it very public. I've seen them in village squares, on the seafront and even in pubs. It's disgusting.

Morris dancers will tell you that they are simply keeping old traditions alive and that Morris Dancing can be traced back to the 15th century. They will proudly tell you that it started as a pagan celebration of spring when local farm workers would blacken their faces with soot so as not to be recognised. They resembled the Moors from North Africa, and so were called Moorish Men or Moorish Dauncers. To be honest who cares where or when it started. I just care about ending it. Morris dancers will tell you that they are actively saving one of our oldest traditions for future generations but I do not believe them for one minute. There is something far more sinister about Morris men and their prancing around like acolytes at a Haitian voodoo ceremony. All that is missing is the sacrifice.

Morris dancing is a ridiculous, unpleasant and dark pastime undertaken by feeble-minded deviants and it must and will be stopped once and for all.

If a recent newspaper report is true it may well be that I do not need to worry about Morris dancers. According to the Morris Ring, which as I am sure you know is the National Association for Men's Morris and Sword Dance Clubs, young people are not joining Morris groups because they are too embarrassed. Now there's a surprise. Why on earth would anyone feel embarrassed at dressing up in coloured rags, blacking their face, covering their arms and legs in bells that have obviously been stolen from cat collars or budgies cages and whirling around like some mad dervish, limp-wristedly waving handkerchiefs in the air while banging the floor with a wooden club crudely decorated with nailed on beer bottle tops – in public. There's nothing embarrassing about that surely.

So, with the average age of a Morris dancer now being 132 and with more and more leaving, as they presumably pass on to the great Morris Ring in the sky, it looks as though they could have all but disappeared in 20 years. Hip hip hooray I say. That's the best news I have read in a long while.

35   Dental Hygienists

I go to a dental hygienist regularly. Her name is Ambrosia but there is nothing sweet or delicious about her. She is a sadist. Before going into her torture chamber I sit in the waiting room, sweating and shaking with fear etched across my face. My instincts are telling me to make a run for the door and to never come back but then common sense kicks in. I know that I'll never get away and that freedom is just an illusion. Like the Canadian Mounties, Ambrosia always gets her man.

When I am in this state another patient will invariably ask me if I am alright and would I like a glass of water. I tell them that I am ok and that I am simply waiting to see Ambrosia. They nod and turn away, barely disguising the look of pity that charged across their face.

As I enter her inner sanctum I always hope that Ambrosia is happy. I pray that she had good sex with one of her girlfriends last night or that this is not a bad time of the month for her. In my naïve mind I think that the happier Ambrosia is the easier my torture will be.

But Ambrosia is not like you and me; I am sure that she is not human. She appears unaffected by emotions and remains dedicated to the task of inflicting as much mental and physical pain on me as she possible can.

I put myself through this twice a year torment because I have been conditioned into believing that it's good for me. Ambrosia has frightened me with stories of people needing to have all of their teeth removed because they failed to regularly visit their hygienist. She has shown me pictures of open mouths with rotting molars and rancid gums, telling me that this is my fate if I stop coming to see her. Ambrosia is a master of the dark arts. She has a PhD in psychological and physical terror.

A session with Ambrosia last around 25 minutes. For each of those 1,500 seconds I am terrified. I am rigid with fright, my hands gripping the arms of the black torture chair until my knuckles are not just white but are close to bursting through the skin which has by then become translucent. I close my eyes so as not to see the delight on her ice-blue eyes as she wields her instruments of torture. Beneath the mask I know that she is licking her lips. And at the end, the thing that annoys me the most, I say "Thank you." Why?

I asked her once why she subjected me to this anguish. Didn't she like me, I asked. She cried, just one tear slowly sliding down her left cheek. She looked at me with anguish in her eyes and gently stroked my face. She told me that it was nothing personal and that she had no feelings for me one way or the other. She just wanted to protect me from the enemy – plaque. She hates plaque. It keeps her awake at night and she is devoting her life to eradicating it from her tiny part of England. The battle is between Ambrosia and the hated plaque and I am just collateral damage.

Despite this unusual show of emotion I still hate her. I pray each night that she will wake up one day forgetting who she is and what her life's work is. Unfortunately my prayers have a habit of not being answered and this is why I am warning Ambrosia and all of her kind. She needs to chill out and find a job that doesn't feed her bitterness towards what is just an aspect of modern day life. It's only plaque for God's sake.

Final Warning

1   Lorry and truck drivers

The one thing that annoys me most about lorry drivers is their lack of respect for other road users, and by that I mean anyone driving anything other than something weighing 15 tons. This shows itself beautifully when you are just about to overtake one of these monsters on a dual carriageway and then they pull out in front of you to overtake the lorry in front of them – and it's uphill. They are barely doing more than one mile per hour more than the lorry in front of them and yet they pull out to overtake. You have to brake and find yourself stuck behind two lorries travelling side by side at a pace that would make a snail look like a Formula 1 car. And it goes on forever.

The lorry on the inside lane doesn't slow down to let the other one in (why should he I suppose) and the one in front of you (the one in the fast overtaking lane) is stuck in no-man's-land. He can't get past the lorry on his left and there's nowhere else to go. He could ease off and pull back behind his lorry-driving buddy but he doesn't. He doggedly stays blocking your lane and remains there until long after the hill has flattened out. It's bloody annoying, it shows a lack of understanding for other road users and it's bad driving. So my message to lorry drivers is "Mend your ways or else – this is your final warning".

2 People who say "There's nothing worse than . . . "

I was having breakfast with a friend once and listened incredulously as he said "There's nothing worse in the world than an underdone egg." Now I hate an undercooked egg as much as the next person but is it the worst thing in the world? "What about Cancer?" I said to him, "That's pretty bad, or having your house destroyed by a lightning strike and then finding out that you forgot to renew the insurance." He got the message. On another occasion I was having a drink with three other friends when one of them uttered the immortal phrase "There's nothing worse than a warm pint." Worse was to come as friend number two chimed in with "Yeah, or stale crisps" while friend number three's contribution was "And what about a pub that doesn't sell crisps at all?" They all nodded in agreement.

I couldn't let it go. I agreed that it was absolutely unacceptable for any pub that we frequent to be guilty of any of these heinous crimes. "We will not give any pub that sells warm beer or stale crisps our custom," I proclaimed. "But in the scheme of things is it worse than being stripped naked, tied to a chair and having an electric cattle prod attached to your genitals?" All three bloody idiots went quiet after that. The problem is that I'm not sure if that was because they were embarrassed and in agreement with what I had just said or if it was because they were simply mulling the question over.

As far as I am concerned there is nothing worse than people saying "There is nothing worse than ....." And it's got to stop now.

3   Drivers of cars with personalised number plates

What is it that makes people want to flaunt their wealth or is it their inadequacy by purchasing a personalised number plate, or as they are referred to in the trade a "cherished" number plate? I haven't seen any statistics showing what the ownership levels are for personalised number plates by different makes of car but I'd bet a tidy sum on BMW drivers being at or close to the top of the list. I was once overtaken by one on a misty pitch black night and all I saw as it disappeared into the murk was the number plate THE 805S with the 8 and the 5 not-too-subtly altered to represent a B and an S. What an utter pillock.

There is definitely a correlation between the cost of the car and the likelihood of it having a personalised number plate. I have never, for example, seen one on a Skoda or on the humble Nissan Micra. The drivers of Porsche, Mercedes, Maserati and Ferrari cars are particularly guilty and over the years I have witnessed a few shockers.

It's bad enough having your name or initials proudly displayed on the front and rear of your car but why does anyone feel the need to put JA62 UAR on their £60,000 plus Jaguar XJ? And why would anyone want to spoil the looks of their absolutely beautiful (and expensive at around £140,000) Aston Martin DB9 with the abominable AST 11N (with the two 1's illegally doctored to look like an 0? Who knows and frankly who cares. The use of personalised number plates is a completely unnecessary display of taste – poor taste. It is ostentatious and it should be abolished. There is one number plate that I have yet to see but somebody must have it somewhere – it epitomises what I feel each and every one of these drivers to be and it's T05 SER.

4   The Clergy

What I particularly dislike about the clergy is that they are always 'there' when there is a disaster or if someone has a personal tragedy. And by 'there' I mean on television, with their smug looking wet face and mealy-mouthed expressions about forgiveness and compassion. Perhaps there is a perfectly good medical reason behind the fact that men of the cloth are so bloody sanctimonious, so forgiving and just damned annoying. Maybe that dog collar that they insist on wearing is constricting the flow of blood to the brain which is therefore stopping them from thinking rationally. On reflection perhaps not. Not all religious men wear a dog collar but they all have that same smug air about them.

When I look around the world at all of the pain and suffering going on (did you see the tears in the eyes of the Sunderland supporters as their team was relegated from the Premier League?) how they can possibly believe that there is some greater being watching over us; an all-knowing and all-powerful God but a God that refuses to step in when things are bad for us. He doesn't sound that bloody good or clever to me.

Let them believe what they want to believe. If they get their kicks out of some misplaced allegiance to an entity that refuses to show himself then fine, but stay away from me and other ordinary folk who are adopting an easy-going approach to life by just trying to get through it on a day to day basis.

They are on a red card, a final warning. They should stop publicly peddling their preposterous faith and get a job like the rest of us. If they fail to heed this warning, and I am pretty sure that they will because they obviously are incapable of using the brain that God gave them, then they will soon be joining some of His other less fortunate creations such as lorry drivers on the Island. There is a danger here of course that they will embrace this with open arms because being placed in a group with others who have been singled out as wrongdoers, misfits or evil deviants is like putting a child in charge of a sweet shop. It's a risk that I am prepared to take for the greater good.

5   Estate Agents

It was a difficult decision as to whether or not estate agents were included in the first tranche of those being deported to the Island. That they missed the cut on this occasion is more down to me wanting to give them one more chance than it is to any failure on their part to meet the criteria. They are on borrowed time and if they want to remain members of society after the revolution they have much to do.

Estate agents must be the most incompetent bunch of 'professionals' that any of us come into contact with. In fact, let's not fool ourselves; they are not 'professional'. Every one of them left school without a single qualification and it was either working as an estate agent or something far more physical like going down the mines. With the UK having no coal mines to speak of, the demand for people to dig out the black stuff has declined and so there is nothing left for these idiots but estate agency. No contest.

They have tried hard to raise the standard of their business and their own reputation by creating what they call *professional bodies* which are supposedly there to set standards and stop bad practice. As far as I can see these bodies are little more than clubs to which you pay a membership fee so that you can put their logo in your window, proving to the general populace that you are a cut above your amateur colleagues. In other words it's nothing more than a con.

Estate agents are despised because of their behaviour, principally because of the language they use to describe properties that they are trying to sell but which are fit only for the bulldozer. If a room is so small that it's impossible to turn around it in it will be described as *bijou*, if they say that the garden is *easily maintained*, you'll know that it's small and largely concrete, and if they describe a property as being in a *sought after area* be prepared to pay a ridiculously high price. The best, of course, is when the agent says *viewing recommended.* On seeing this sentence you should walk away and don't stop until your shoes have worn out. This epithet is only used for the ugliest house on the street, the house that only a desperate idiot would buy and a house that is totally un-sellable.

Estate agents lack any ethics whatsoever. They will 'accidentally' arrange two viewings at the same time to show you how popular the property is with the underlying message being if you want it you must put in an offer immediately. They are unscrupulous and will do anything for the sale and their commission. With the increasing use of the Internet, the high street estate agents days are probably numbered anyway but, like vermin, they have a habit of surviving. But if they fail to change their ways their survival is limited; they will be in the next group to be go across the water to their new home.

6   Fat People

Some people have said to me that I shouldn't hate fat people because it's not their fault. They tell me that I should feel sorry for them and just be glad that I am not one of them. At times when I have had nothing to do I've given this notion some thought and have asked myself if I am being cruel. Perhaps I am. Perhaps it's in their genes and there but for the grace of God go I. And then I get behind one at the checkout of our local supermarket and watch as they take their goods from the trolley and put them on the conveyor belt.

Three huge deep pan pizzas (quattro formaggio of course), two large pots of full fat Greek yoghurt, 18 packets of crisps, a monstrous lump of cheddar cheese, a bag of French fries emblazoned with the caption 50% extra Free, and a pack of six cream doughnuts. And at the end, no doubt to somehow assuage their guilt, a couple of large bottles of Diet Coke.

How could I possibly think that they were not to blame for the fact that they had an ass the size of an elephant's rear end or rolls of fat that would shame a sumo wrestler? Of course it's their bloody fault, the fat greedy bastards. No one is forcing them to buy and eat this crap. It's their choice and they must surely know what the consequences are of eating 200 grams of fat a day. They ought to know; it's staring them in the face every time they look in a mirror or get dressed.

I am very aware that weight is a big issue particularly with young girls where body image has become the overriding factor that drives their lives. I also understand the danger of concentrating too much on not being fat and I am certainly not advocating that we all starve ourselves to thinness.

I also accept that each and every one of us can do what the hell we like in terms of what we eat and that we shouldn't think any less of anyone just because of the way they look. But being fat, and by fat I mean obese, so grossly overweight that you can't tie up your shoes, cut your toenails or walk more than a couple of hundred yards uphill without being out of breath, is not good for you.

Some fat people, like Mrs Scady, tell me that they like being the way they are. These are the same people who talk shit. No one likes being so overweight that it affects their life. I can't see the fun in being so big that you take up two seats on a bus or a train or that you find it impossible to squeeze yourself into a seat on an aeroplane. No one wants to be so big that they can't walk normally, so they have to waddle around like some gigantic duck-like creature because their thighs are so gross that every time they put one foot in front of the other all you can hear is the sound of two great lumps of fat hitting each other. And taking it to the extreme, no one wants to be so fat that they can't move from their home because they just don't have the strength to move their heavy weight around.

Fat people should not be pitied and they should not be accepted. Being fat is avoidable and what is needed is some honesty. Fat people need to admit that they are fat, that they get no pleasure from being like it and that the reason that they are like it is because they eat too much fatty food. Put simply they are lard buckets. If they fail then I am sorry to say that they will find that the issue will be taken out of their control and they will face the dawn walk to the ferry, or more like waddle, whether they like it or not.

7   German Tourists

They are renowned for their rudeness and their arrogance. Who else but a Kraut would even bother to get up when everyone else is going to bed just so that they can place their towels on the sunbeds around the pool and thus bag them for the rest of the day. And what about their behaviour in the hotel restaurant? Talk about pigs with their snouts in the trough. They push, they elbow and they stand solid to stop anyone else, particularly the Brits, from getting anywhere near the food. My tactic in this situation is to simply whistle a favourite song from the Second World War, the one about old Adolf being challenged in the testicular department. For those who don't know it here are the words of the two most popular versions.

Hitler has only got one ball
Göring has got two but they're very small
Himmler has something sim'lar
But poor old Goebbels has no balls at all
Hitler has only got one ball
The other is in the Albert Hall
His mother, the dirty bugger
Cut it off when he was small

It's not the words that are important, however, it's the tune. I guarantee that no matter how young they are the Germans in the queue ahead of you will recognise this instantly. When I deploy this, my favourite weapon, the Germans in my sights will always glare at me in that Teutonic way that they have. They will be visibly fuming as the anger and hatred pours from their puce faces. I simply smile and say *Good morning* and then sotto voce . . . *Fritz.* Bad though they are, German tourists have escaped – this time – but only because there is so much competition and also because I will get far more pleasure in continuing to taunt them than I would by removing them altogether. They are, however, along with a few others on a final warning.

8 Walkers

I love walking. I particularly love walking on wild moorland or along the coast with the wind in my face and just a few birds wheeling overhead for company. There are few things better than being alone with nature to stir the soul and recharge the batteries that have been depleted by the daily grind of life. But I hate walkers. Not all walkers. I don't hate myself for instance. My hatred is reserved for the idiots who believe that to enjoy a walk you need to be better equipped than a Royal Marine Commando about to embark on a 40 mile yomp into enemy territory.

The walkers I am talking about are the ones with sticks and boots, and hanging on a red cord around their neck a compass and an OS map in a see-through pouch. I detest them. And if they are also wearing a baseball cap with a flap at the back, presumably to protect their pathetic shrivelled neck from being burned by the intolerably fierce English sun, then I detest them even more. The only thing worse than meeting one of these walkers is meeting a group of them. This is when the pillock at the front shouts out "Car" every time one approaches.

Why can't they just enjoy a walk in the countryside like the rest of us? Why do they have to dress up as if they are about to climb Mt Everest? I have no idea and to be honest I don't care. I am warning them loud and clear; they need to get rid of the compass and all of the other utterly useless accoutrements and just enjoy a walk like the rest of us. If they don't then their very last walk here among the rest of us will be a very short one and they will certainly not need a map, sticks or a stupid hat to help them on their way.

9   People with tattoos or body piercing

The origin of body piercing and tattooing can be traced back some 5,000 years but their current popularity is a relatively recent phenomenon. With regard to the disgusting practice of tattoos there is just one person to blame for their widespread acceptance and that is David Beckham. BB (Before Beckham) the only people who were stupid enough to have a tattoo were soldiers, sailors, drunks, convicts and anyone else with an IQ of less than 12; coincidentally this is also the average IQ of the common woodlouse. As for piercings the blame for their popularity can be traced back to the punk movement of the 1970's when large groups of inadequates were feted by a music industry in decline and allowed to release one moronic song after another, preaching anarchy and proudly displaying noses, ears, nipples and other appendages pierced with the common or garden safety pin.

Tattoos are not pretty and they are not sexy and, as I have said, BB they were the undeniable preserve of the lower class but because of the boy wonder from Essex this exclusivity no longer exists. At one stage even the then Prime Minister's wife (the not-so-lovely Sam Cam) had a tattoo, albeit a small blue dolphin on her ankle. There is nothing on record of her ever having a body piercing but I have it on good authority that she succumbed to Dave's wishes that she also have a certain part of her body decorated with a gold pin in the shape of the Tory torch, just to show that she was an ordinary person. And there's the irony because ordinary, normal people do not have tattoos or body piercings (other than for earrings).

The only people who disfigure their bodies with these hideous adornments are social inadequates; desperate people who believe that a tattoo of a butterfly on their right breast or a cheap ring through their lip, nose or eyelid somehow shows the world that they are hip, cool or on-trend or whatever the current terminology is to describe something that is deemed ultra-fashionable. They are wrong of course. They are stupid and they are on a warning.

10   Americans and Australians

And last, but by no means least, Americans - those great people from across the *pond* as they irritatingly insist on calling the second largest ocean in the world - and Australians. It saddens me to give our English speaking friends, cousins and allies from these two wonderful countries a final warning but they leave me no choice.

The Americans have always been a self-righteous, God-fearing lot with an ego the size of their country but that hardly warrants their expulsion to the Isle of Wight. What does, however, is Donald Trump. He represents all that I detest about his country: he is big, brash, bullying and bigoted. On my only trip to America I was impressed by the way that American women fell at my feet in adoration just because I was speaking with that 'cute English accent', and, to tell the truth, I've often wished I'd married an American woman; they have just a bit more style and pizazz than Mrs Scady. However, their choice of a semi-literate, egotistical, fields-of-barley-headed, 'bad person' of a President has somewhat diminished my affection for the US of A. His actions are putting his whole nation at risk and my suggestion to all Americans would be to get him out, one way or the other, as soon as possible. Only then will the inhabitants of this beautiful country be safe.

As for Australians, it's a no-brainer really. They are already kindred spirits of those who live on the Isle of Wight with both being descended from a similar criminal heritage. I suppose I shouldn't blame them for their ancestry, but I do blame them for being so damned upbeat and laid-back about everything, not to mention the fact that they enjoy glorious weather at Christmas whilst I have to shiver away with Mrs Scady's relatives.

And speaking of Mrs Scady we recently had two Australian young men stay with us, *friends* that Mrs Scady and I met whilst on holiday in Greece. Throughout their stay they complained about the small size of our house, our car and our roads. They even criticised our choice of television viewing and would evict us from our own settee if there was something that they wanted to watch. They were rude about our beer and our cricket team but I noticed that they had a certain fondness for our women-folk. It used to be said of the Americans that they were over-sexed, over-paid and over here. I fear that this description now applies to Australian men. After the departure of our two Antipodean guests Mrs Scady discovered 14 apple cores, the remains of three steak and kidney pies and a *girlie* magazine under their beds.

For this alone they very nearly condemned their fellow countrymen to the Island but in line with my innate generosity of spirit I am simply giving them a final warning. Improve, or else.

.

A word from the author

The working title for this book was originally *First Against The Wall* and as the name suggests the worthless reprobates described herein were to receive a fate far worse than simply being deported to the Isle of Wight.

They were to have been marched out from their dank cells at dawn, blindfolded and stood against the wall. There they would wait, some in anticipation, some in fear and some no doubt with a smug know-it-all look upon their pathetic faces, for the handpicked firing squad to carry out their duty.

Those of you, like me, who have some knowledge of the IOW, may consider that death is by far the better option.

Mrs Scady, being somewhat more understanding of human nature and certainly more forgiving of human frailties than I am, persuaded me that this was, however, a little excessive. I remain to be convinced.

Acknowledgements

I must give my thanks to Mrs Scady for encouraging me to write this book. During the darkest hours when the writers' block descended like a theatre fire curtain it was Mrs Scady who insisted I continue writing. Come rain or shine and for one extended period during January, heavy snow, she would march me down to my shed at the end of the garden. This was my writing den. As the door closed and I heard Mrs Scady closing the padlock I set about my task.

I owe a depth of gratitude to Mrs Scady for reading my early proofs, correcting my schoolboy English, providing feedback, for the cover design and for the marketing and publicity associated with this book. It was Mrs Scady who curbed my sometimes over-enthusiastic language and who kept me supplied with copious amounts of red wine. She has worked tirelessly to ensure that this book was finished, at one time even leaving our lovely home in Dorset to stay with some holiday friends in Inverness for three months so that I could write with no distractions.

About the author, Colin Scady

Colin Scady has a BA (Hons) from Bournemouth University where he gained a reputation for being a know-it-all and drunk.

This is Colin's first published work; he has five other books gathering dust on the shelves of his ramshackle house on the Dorset coast. He lives there with his long-suffering wife; it's not known how long the marriage will last if she gets to read this, his latest tome. Colin likes to spend time criticising others and striving for unpopularity wherever he goes. He is a member of his local Parish Council and unsurprisingly six other members resigned on the day he was appointed. He is a thorn in the side of all those he meets.

Colin has a number of idiosyncrasies not the least of which are his sense of fashion and colour coordination. He has neither. It is no coincidence that Colin Scady has several ex-wives and that he spent 20 years living alone, getting to know his unfortunate self. As you will by now have gathered, he is a bigoted megalomaniac and a spiteful misanthrope. His cup is always half empty and he spends his life 'looking for the bad' in others.

When asked to describe her husband Mrs Scady said 'He is bossy, opinionated, mean-spirited, offensive, embarrassing and hell to live with. In all other ways he is the perfect husband."

24692731R00153

Printed in Great Britain
by Amazon